I0661786

I DO, FOR NOW

CHRISTY MCKELLEN

Boldwood

First published in 2018 as *A Contract, A Wedding, A Wife*. This edition published in Great Britain in 2025 by Boldwood Books Ltd.

Copyright © Christy McKellen, 2018

Cover Design by Leah Jacobs-Gordon

Cover Images: Leah Jacobs-Gordon

The moral right of Christy McKellen to be identified as the author of this work has been asserted in accordance with the Copyright, Designs and Patents Act 1988.

All rights reserved. No part of this book may be reproduced in any form or by any electronic or mechanical means, including information storage and retrieval systems, without written permission from the author, except for the use of brief quotations in a book review. This book is a work of fiction and, except in the case of historical fact, any resemblance to actual persons, living or dead, is purely coincidental.

Every effort has been made to obtain the necessary permissions with reference to copyright material, both illustrative and quoted. We apologise for any omissions in this respect and will be pleased to make the appropriate acknowledgements in any future edition.

A CIP catalogue record for this book is available from the British Library.

Paperback ISBN 978-1-83617-116-4

Large Print ISBN 978-1-83617-115-7

Hardback ISBN 978-1-83617-114-0

Trade Paperback ISBN 978-1-80656-063-9

Ebook ISBN 978-1-83617-117-1

Kindle ISBN 978-1-83617-118-8

Audio CD ISBN 978-1-83617-109-6

MP3 CD ISBN 978-1-83617-110-2

Digital audio download ISBN 978-1-83617-112-6

This book is printed on certified sustainable paper. Boldwood Books is dedicated to putting sustainability at the heart of our business. For more information please visit https://www.boldwoodbooks.com/about-us/sustainability/

Boldwood Books Ltd, 23 Bowerdean Street, London, SW6 3TN

www.boldwoodbooks.com

1

RISK – A GAME OF STRATEGY, CONFLICT AND DIPLOMACY.

He was never going to find someone suitable to marry at this rate.

Xavier McQueen let out an exasperated sigh as the woman who had seemed like his best hope – on paper at least – gave a firm and very final 'no' to his admittedly completely barmy-sounding proposal before putting the phone down on him.

Apparently, only being married for a year before divorcing wouldn't look good on her dating CV. She was under the impression it could put off real prospects in the future because they'd be worried about her coming with baggage from such a short previous marriage.

Closing his eyes, he slumped back in his chair.

Three months he'd been wasting his time with this ridiculous endeavour and now he only had six weeks left before the Hampstead mansion where he'd lived for the last four years – the home that had been in his family for the last hundred and fifty years – would pass to his money-grubbing clown of a cousin.

Damn his great-aunt and her jeopardous eccentricity.

He thought she'd loved him – certainly more than his parents ever had – but this bizarre stunt she'd pulled with her will had made him wonder about that.

Shoving a hand through his hair and trying not to pull it out in his frustration, he stared out of the floor-to-ceiling window of his office, barely registering his view of the majestic Tower Bridge stretching out across the fast-moving River Thames.

He'd not wanted to widely advertise exactly what he was looking for in case it brought out the crooks and the crazies, but that meant he'd quickly run out of people to ask to help him out. The problem was, the chosen candidate needed to be someone he could trust, as well as someone he'd be able to get along with, but all his good female friends were already married, and he didn't fancy taking his chances with any of his exes. A year was a long time to live with someone who detested the very sight of you.

The other two women, who had also been put forward as possible candidates by his friend Russell – the only friend he'd trusted with his problem – hadn't worked out either. Not being able to have sex for a year hadn't appealed to either of them. They'd both been looking for the real deal. Soul mates. An ideal he had no faith in whatsoever any more, not after being left humiliated at the altar five years ago by the woman he'd thought he'd spend the rest of his life with. His disaster of a non-wedding, which he now liked to think of as a near miss, had put paid to that ridiculous notion.

Nope, it was short-term, uncomplicated relationships for him from here on in. Or a purely business one like this needed to be, thanks to the bizarre demands stipulated in Great-Aunt Faith's will.

Just as he was reaching for the glass of water on his desk to relieve his parched throat, there was a loud knock on the door and a petite woman with bright blue eyes and a riot of blonde curls walked purposefully into his office and placed a small basket of assorted cakes on his desk with a flourish.

He frowned down at them, then up at her. 'I didn't order any cakes.'

'I know. They're an excuse to get some face-to-face time with you,' she said, folding her arms and looking down at him with a determined expression that made his stomach sink.

'I've been trying to get a meeting with you for weeks, but your PA keeps fobbing me off,' she went on before he had a chance to say anything. 'So, I've been forced to take drastic action. On the other hand, I've brought you some really fantastic cakes. I made them myself. So it's actually a win for you.' She flashed him a half-smile that didn't entirely convince him she was as self-assured as her spirited speech had made her seem.

He leant back in his chair again and studied her in bemusement.

She looked young, maybe early-to-mid-twenties, with a sweetly pretty face.

Her abundance of curly blonde hair, which she'd tried to tame with an Alice band, stuck out around her head, probably due to the windy day. She surveyed him back with intelligent eyes, her button nose, which was scattered with freckles, wrinkling a little under his gaze. She seemed to him to have the air of someone who could cause a great deal of mischief if she put her mind to it.

As he scrutinised her, she shifted on the spot and visibly swallowed, as if rapidly losing her nerve in the face of his silence. It seemed her blustery, confident entrance had all been an act to get past the temporary PA sitting outside his office. Soon to be his ex-temporary PA.

'And you are?' he said with a sigh. He really didn't need this extra hassle today; his nerves were already strung as tightly as they'd go, and he had an important meeting in ten minutes which he needed to have his head in the game for.

'Solitaire Saunders. Soli for short. That's what everyone ends up calling me, anyway. It's a bit of a mouthful otherwise.'

His eyebrow twitched involuntarily upwards.

'Solitaire? Like the diamond?'

She gave a self-conscious grin. 'No, like the card game. My dad was a huge fan of games. He set up our board game cafe on Hampstead High Street – in the unit we rent from your company.'

Board game cafe?

He was surprised anyone could make a living from a business like that, though, judging by the increasingly irate letters he now remembered receiving from the woman running the place – presumably this woman – after they'd notified her of the upcoming rent raise, perhaps she didn't.

Despite his reluctance to get into this with her right now, he knew he ought to nip the issue in the bud while she was here in front of him. His personal assistant was fed up with having to field her constant phone calls asking to speak to him directly and he'd never been one to shy away from a legitimate business conflict when it reared its head. Its pretty, curly blonde head in this instance.

'The trouble is, Soli,' he said, splaying his hands on the desktop, 'the market's moved on a lot since you last signed the rental agreement a couple of years ag—'

'Four years ago,' she butted in. 'And it was my father who signed it. I've been running it without him for the last three of them.'

'Okay, I don't have the exact details to hand right now,' he said, trying to remain patient, 'but I do know that the market's moved even more since then.' He lifted his hands, palms towards her. 'We're not monsters here, we've actually held back on increasing the rent on a lot of our property because we know how hard it can be for small independent businesses to survive in London, but we have to move with the times.'

'You know how hard it is to run a struggling business, do you?' she shot back. 'How utterly heartbreaking it is when a once thriving business starts to fail? How demoralising that can be?' Her voice rose on each question. She glanced pointedly around his plush office with its high-end furniture and enviable London view then fixed him with a challenging look, her cheeks flushed a deep shade of pink but the expression in her eyes was unwavering.

He experienced a shiver of guilt but knew he couldn't let it get to him. Everyone he came across these days seemed to have a sob story to tell him so that he'd agree to charge them less money for the property they rented from his company. He couldn't let his personal feelings get in the way. This was business.

'We live above the cafe,' she said before he could form his careful reply. 'If we can't afford to keep the business going, we'll lose our home as well, but then I don't expect you'd know how a threat like that feels either!'

If only that were the case.

He began to shake his head, but she took a step closer to his desk and put her hands over her heart, her cute little nose wrinkling again in a way that made something twist uncomfortably in his chest.

'Is there any way I can persuade you to hold off for a little while longer?' she asked in a voice wobbly with emotion. 'Please. Just give me a chance to get a bit more business in.'

'How do you intend to do that?' he asked, genuinely interested. 'Aren't there a lot of other cafe options on Hampstead High Street?'

Her bold stance deflated a little. 'Yes. Unfortunately, there are. But they're mostly chains owned by big corporations.' She waved a dismissive hand. 'We offer a more local, family-run atmosphere. And board games! Who doesn't love playing board games?'

He shuffled a little in his chair. 'Can't say I'm a huge fan of them.'

'You just haven't played the right ones yet,' she persisted. 'If you come in, you'll see how much fun they can be. We have four hundred games to choose from. Something for everyone. We'll even teach you how to play them.'

He shook his head, holding back the smile that was pushing at the corners of his mouth. Learning to play board games was the last thing he could imagine wanting to do with his precious time off. 'As appealing as that sounds,' he said, trying to keep the irony out of his voice, 'that doesn't tell me how you're going to start making enough profit to pay your rent.'

'I'm working on it,' she stated, but her gaze wasn't meeting his now; instead, she was staring out towards the river, her hands clenched at her sides as if she was fighting to keep her composure. 'I just need to find some time to do a bit of local advertising, update the website and post to the social media sites we're on,' she said, almost to herself. 'Trouble is, I work long hours. I have a cleaning job at a gastropub from seven-thirty till ten, then I have to make the cakes and prepare the sandwiches we sell at the cafe, then we're open from eleven till three. When we close, I have to go shopping for supplies for both the cafe and the family and take care of anything my mum needs and then the cafe's open again from 5 till 10 p.m. So there's not been a lot of time for developing a high-concept business strategy.'

More guilt tried to shoulder its way in as she looked back at him with tired eyes.

He shook it off. This wasn't his problem. He couldn't allow it to become his problem either. He had enough of his own troubles to deal with right now.

'Look, Soli, things are complicated for me at the moment, and I'm afraid I don't have time to deal with this today. I have an important meeting in a few minutes, so if you leave your contact details with my PA—'

She flinched at the hard edge he'd given his voice now, but didn't move from where she stood.

'Complicated? You think your life's complicated? Beat this, buster.' She pointed her finger at him. 'I'm desperately trying to save the business my late father built from scratch, our family's legacy, so I can afford to get my mother, who's suffering with Parkinson's disease, the care she needs whilst also trying to scrape together enough money to support my younger sister, who's a brilliant mathematician with an offer from Oxford University, but who can't afford to take the place there. And you're making it even harder for me to do all that by raising our already extortionate rent. That's complicated!'

The ensuing silence rang out loudly in the still air of his office.

'Okay. Fine,' he said resignedly when he saw a glint of tears in her eyes. 'You win the "complicated" competition.' He made a placating gesture. 'But only just – believe me. My life isn't exactly easy right now either.'

'Look, is there some sort of arrangement we could come to here?' she asked desperately, blinking back her tears and looking a little embarrassed about losing her cool. 'Any sort of deal we could make which would give me a bit more time to try and turn the fortunes of the cafe around and make the money we need to afford the rent hike? I can't lose the place. Not after all the love and hard graft my father put into it. It's all we have left of him now.' Despite her efforts, a single tear ran down her cheek.

He looked hurriedly away, frowning down at his desk. 'I've already held back on rolling out the new rent and if I do it for you, I'll have to—'

'Please. Have a heart,' she broke in hoarsely, clearly aware she was losing the battle but seemingly not prepared to accept it. 'I'll do anything. I'll come and work here for you when I'm not working at the cafe. I can type and make coffee, file things. Documents. Tidy up! I'll do whatever it takes to keep our cafe running.'

The ring of hope in her voice clawed at his chest. He had to give her credit; she was certainly determined.

Or maybe just desperate.

His heart gave a hard thump. He knew what desperate felt like and he wouldn't wish it on anyone.

'Whatever it takes?' he asked slowly, meeting her eyes again now. He wasn't sure where he was going with this, but he had the strangest feeling there could be a solution here that he hadn't quite hit upon yet.

'Anything. Just name it,' she said, her eyes wide with anticipation.

He sighed and shook his head. 'The thing is, I have a PA already. There wouldn't be anything for you to do here at the office.'

'At your house, then? I'm a great cleaner. Fast and totally reliable.'

'Got a whole team of those.'

'Then what do you need? There has to be something.'

And there it was.

The idea.

But he couldn't suggest that.

Could he?

No.

He shouldn't.

'Please,' she whispered in a broken voice, tears brimming in her eyes again.

'What I need most right now is a wife,' he said roughly, losing the grip on his restraint as the idea pushed harder at his brain and compassion loosened his tongue. 'At least, I need to find a woman that's prepared to get married in the next few weeks and stay married to me for a year.' Catching the expression of shock on her face, he silently cursed himself for letting that slip out.

She must think he was a total loony.

'Are you serious?' she asked in a faltering voice.

He sighed, feeling tiredness wash through him. 'Unfortunately, I am.'

'Why do you need a wife so fast?'

'Like I said, it's complicated.'

She surprised him by perching on the edge of his desk and fixing him with an intent stare. 'Well, you listened to my problems; let me hear yours.'

His pulse stuttered. 'I don't think it's appropriate—'

She held up her hands in a halting motion. 'Just tell me. Perhaps I can help.'

He frowned at her, taken aback by her unexpected forcefulness. 'I very much doubt it.'

'Look, I won't say anything to anyone if that's what you're worried about. I'm good with secrets. Maybe it would help to say it all out loud. That's what my dad used to do. He used me as a sounding board and often I didn't need to say a word: he already had the answer; he was just having trouble accessing it.'

He took a moment to study her, trying to judge whether he could trust her not to blab to all and sundry once she'd left his office. The last thing he needed right now was for this to be circulated around social media or the press. He was already taking enough risks talking to the women he'd approached so far, and it could only be a matter of time before his luck ran out.

'Go on. What harm can it do?' she murmured, giving him a reassuring smile. There was something about her that encouraged confidences, he realised, and for some reason he felt, deep down, that he could trust her.

He sighed, deciding that he may as well tell her the whole sorry tale since she knew most of it already anyway. Plus, he didn't really have anything more to lose at this point. And who knew, perhaps she could help in some way?

Stranger things had happened.

Getting up from his chair, he paced over to the window and stared out at the pleasure boats transporting tourists up and down the wide river. 'My late great-aunt owned the house I live in at the moment.' He swallowed past the dryness in his throat. 'It's the place I've considered to be my home for my entire life. It was meant to go to my father next, but he passed away a few years ago, so I'm next in line to inherit it,' he said, glancing back to check she was listening.

She was. She gazed back at him with an open, interested expression, her hands folded neatly in her lap.

'It's been in my family since 1875, ever since it was built for my great-great-grandfather,' he continued, turning back to look at the river again. 'It's the house where I spent all my holidays from boarding school and the home I intend to live in until I die.' He paused for a moment, feeling his throat tighten as he remembered how he used to say it was the place where he and Harriet would always live, before – well, before his whole life was turned upside down.

Shaking off the tension this memory produced, he moved away from the window and sat back down on his chair.

'In order to inherit the place, though, a covenant in the will states I have to be married within the next month.' He tried not to grimace as he said it.

She nodded slowly. 'Okay.' Frowning now as if a little puzzled, she said, 'Could I just ask – why the rush? Haven't you known about this for a while?'

'No. Apparently my great-aunt wrote it into her will a couple of years ago, but she was in a coma for eighteen months after suffering a massive stroke. I only found out about it three months ago when she passed away.'

He paused and swallowed, shaking his head as a wave of sadness at losing the woman he thought of as more of a mother figure than a great-aunt flooded through him. 'I only inherit it if I'm married by my thirtieth birthday and remain married for at least a year, otherwise it gets passed on to my cousin, who is already married.' He grimaced. 'And the most immoral, wasteful, tasteless man I've ever met. He'd sell the place to the highest bidder in the blink of an eye.'

There was a heavy pause where he watched her eyes widen and her mouth twitch at the corner.

'And before you ask, no, he wouldn't sell it to me. We don't exactly get on.'

'I kind of gathered that from your description of him,' she said with a smile.

He tried to smile back but he couldn't quite muster the energy needed. Mirth was a hard response to summon when you were about to lose the only place in the world that really meant something to you. The place that held all your childhood memories and felt like an integral part of your history.

Your home.

He'd feel baseless without it, adrift, disenfranchised.

'Well,' she said, her eyes alive with what looked suspiciously like amusement, 'that's quite a conundrum you have there. It's like something from a soap opera.' Her mouth twitched. 'And not a very good one.'

Rubbing his hand over his brow, he felt the tension this predicament had caused under his fingertips. 'I'd have to agree with you.'

'Your great-aunt sounds like a real character.' Her eyes still sparkled with amusement, but her smile was warm.

'She was a little eccentric, yes.'

Crossing her arms, she peered down at him. 'And I'm guessing no one you've asked so far has said yes to this rather unusual proposal?'

'Correct. Not that there have been many suitable candidates.' He leant back in his chair and mirrored her by crossing his own arms. 'The fact we'd have to live together to make it look like we're a real couple – apparently a solicitor will be deployed at random times to check on this,' he added by way of explanation, 'but not have a real relationship hasn't exactly caught the attention of the women I've approached so far. I'm really only interested in getting married as a business arrangement; I'm not looking for true love.'

Her brow furrowed at this. 'You don't want to fall in love?'

'No.'

There was a small pause before she asked, 'Why not?'

He shrugged. 'It's just not for me, that's all. Despite my great-aunt's insistence that it was the best thing that ever happened to her, I don't believe falling in love with someone can really make you happy.' He sat up in his chair. 'In fact, I think it does the opposite. It didn't work out for my parents, or for a large population of the country, and I intend to learn from their mistakes.'

Not to mention his own near miss – though he wasn't about to tell her about that humiliating experience.

'Just out of interest, what does your temporary bride get out of this arrangement?' she asked in a faltering voice, jerking him out of his scrambled thoughts.

There was a tense pause where they looked at each other and he weighed up what he'd be prepared to offer her if she meant what he thought she meant by that.

'The candidate would be able to keep the rental cost on their property the same for the next five years,' he replied slowly.

'And would there be some sort of pay-out as soon as she'd signed the marriage register?' she asked, her gaze intent on his now.

'There could be, if it was a reasonable request.'

'But she'd have to live with you,' she appeared to swallow, 'in your house?'

Noting the renewed flush of her skin, he could guess what she actually meant by that.

'It would be a purely business arrangement,' he reassured her, 'which would mean she'd sleep in her own bedroom. There wouldn't be any conjugal expectations. In fact, it would be a totally platonic relationship, to avoid any complications.'

'I see,' she said, her shoulders seeming to relax a little.

Despite his wish to keep sex out of the deal, he couldn't help but feel a little miffed by her apparent horror at the idea of sleeping with him. Was it really that off-putting an idea? He shook off his irritation, telling himself not to be an idiot. The woman didn't know him from the next man, so of course she'd be nervous about the idea of any expected intimacy between them.

'We'd also both have to agree not to have any sexual relationships outside the marriage, again, to avoid complications.'

'Okay,' she said without expression, not giving him any clues about her feelings on that one. Would that be a deal-breaker for her? She was an attractive, sparky woman and he guessed she must get plenty of male attention. There was something really appealing about her, especially when she smiled.

'One of the other stipulations would be that she'd need to take my surname for the duration of the marriage,' he said, pulling his attention back to the matter at hand. 'It would just be for appearances, and she could change it back again afterwards, of course.'

'Afterwards?'

'After the divorce. There'll be a pre-nuptial agreement to sign so she won't be able to petition for money or property during the legal severance of the marriage.'

There was a pause in which the air seemed to vibrate between them.

'Oka-a-ay,' she said slowly, her voice sounding a little breathy now.

He frowned, panicking for moment that she might be stringing him along for a laugh.

Before he could start to backpedal, though, she fixed him with a steady gaze, her lips quirking into a wide smile – triggering a warm, lifting sensation of hope in his chest – then took an audible breath and said, 'I'll do it. I'll be your wife.'

2

MONOPOLY – MOVE AROUND THE BOARD FOR THE CHANCE TO COLLECT MONEY AND NEW PROPERTY.

Solitaire Saunders heard her father's voice in her head as she gazed anxiously back at the man who had the power to turn the course of her and her family's lives around with a mere nod.

'Your tendency to run headlong into things without thinking is going to get you in serious trouble some day, Soli,' her father's voice warned her.

He wasn't wrong.

She knew that.

But you're not here any more, Dad, and I'm doing the best I can.

There was a chance, of course, that she was actually dreaming all this and would wake up at any moment in bed with her heart racing and her palms as sweaty as they felt right now.

But she really hoped that wasn't the case.

In fact, she knew it wasn't possible because when she'd actually rolled out of bed this morning and been unable to eat her breakfast because her stomach was jumping around so badly with nerves and worry, she'd never felt so awake – and afraid. The pressure of her mum and sister relying on her to stop both their home and livelihoods from being swept out from under them weighed heavily on her.

So she was hyper-aware, sitting there now in her smartest clothes with her wild hair as neat as she'd been able to get it, that how well she performed in this meeting could change all their lives for ever, one way or another. What she hadn't expected when she turned up here was to be confronted with such an unusual and nerve-racking way to do it.

This – this incredible stroke of luck – could be the answer to all her problems.

If she could handle it, that was.

As far as she could see, the most challenging thing about it would be having to see Xavier McQueen, property baron and high-society mover and shaker every day for the next year.

And be his wife.

The thought of living with this powerful, domineering stranger made her heart thump harder in her chest.

The guy was seriously attractive, with a lean but muscular physique which she imagined he kept looking that fit with regular trips to the gym. His face was angular, with high cheekbones and a strong jaw, and he had light green, almond-shaped eyes, framed with dark lashes, which gave him a nerve-jangling look of stark intensity. And he had really good hair. Thick and shiny and the colour of melted chocolate. It sat neatly against his scalp as if it had been styled deliberately to do that by a master hairdresser at a top salon. Which, she mused, it probably had. Her fingers twitched at her sides as she fought a powerful urge to reach out and touch the soft waves, to see if it was as soft and smooth as it looked.

'I have some non-negotiable demands if I'm going to do this,' she said, a little more loudly than she'd meant to out of nerves.

'I thought you might have,' Xavier replied, with an ironic tinge to his voice. He had to be the most sardonic person she'd ever met. Throughout all their exchanges it had seemed as though he'd been having trouble taking anything she'd said seriously.

Still, he wasn't exactly laughing now. In fact, despite his sarcasm, he was actually looking at her as if she might be the answer to all his problems.

'Okay. If I'm going to be your wife for a year, I need to know that my mother is being taken care of properly, so I'll need to have a live-in carer provided for her while I'm away. She'll be mostly okay during the day, but she'll definitely need someone there overnight to help her get ready for bed and to get up when my sister's not there. Which leads me on to the next stipulation. I also want you to pay for my sister's living expenses while she's at university.' Her heart was racing as she laid all this out, wondering whether he'd just tell her to get up and get out because she was being too greedy.

But he needs you, a voice in the back of her head told her, so front it out.

There was a long pause while he looked at her with such an intense gaze she felt it right down to her toes.

'Okay, so let me get this straight,' he said eventually; 'you want a full-time carer for your mother, living expenses paid for your sister, a stay on the rent on the cafe for the next five years and an as yet undisclosed sum of money as soon as we're married?'

She swallowed hard, but held her nerve. 'Yes.'

'And how much were you thinking of for your lump sum?'

Shakily, she said an amount that she thought would cover the wages at the cafe for the next year as well as giving her some spending money which she could use for marketing or renovations to the cafe once they were divorced.

He surveyed her for a moment, his right eyebrow twitching upwards by a couple of degrees.

Soli held her breath, aware of her pulse throbbing in her head.

Had she blown it by asking for too much?

'Okay. It's a deal,' he said finally. 'But, considering you'll be losing your wage from the cleaning job and you'll have to employ someone to cover your position in the cafe, I'm prepared to give you an additional 20 per cent on top of that.'

Soli swallowed hard, his unexpected generosity bringing tears to her eyes.

'As long as you agree to marry to me within the next month and spend the majority of your time in my home,' he added quickly. 'I don't mind you visiting your mother and working part-time at the cafe, perhaps one or two days a week so you can keep an eye on it, but it needs to look as though the majority of your time is spent living there with me. Particularly in the evenings.'

'So I can only work during the day?'

'Yes. I'd like it if you were able to attend any work or social events at the drop of a hat. For that, I need you focused on your life with me as much as possible.'

She suspected that what he wasn't saying out loud was that he wasn't the sort of man to have the owner of a board game cafe for a wife and he didn't want to have to explain himself to anyone.

'So what will I do for the rest of the time?' she asked as indignation rippled through her. What was wrong with working in a board game cafe? She really enjoyed it. It was sociable and kept her fit because she was on her feet all day.

He frowned, momentarily stumped by her question. 'Perhaps you could work on that "high-concept business strategy" you haven't had time for?' He waved a hand. 'I'm sure you'll find plenty of things to do with your day.'

'And what do you want me to tell people when they ask what I do for a living?' she asked, still riled by her suspicion that he didn't value her choice of livelihood. 'What do the kind of women you normally date do for a job?' she added, perhaps a little tetchily.

He rubbed a hand over his forehead, looking taken aback by the directness of her question. 'Most of the women I've dated have either had a media job or been a doctor or solicitor.'

'Well, I don't think I'm going to convince anyone I'm a doctor or lawyer,' Soli said, raising a wry eyebrow. 'My sister got all the brains in the family.'

He frowned, apparently a little bemused by her now. 'Okay, well, if you want to choose a different career for yourself, go right ahead. What would you have done if you hadn't taken over the cafe? Do you have any burning ambitions?'

His question stumped her for a second. It had been a long time since she'd thought about doing anything but running the cafe. 'I don't know. I wasn't exactly focused at school so I never expected to have a high-flying career. I liked designing clothes, but I did that in my spare time. My dad pressganged me into taking academic subjects to "give me a better chance in life".' She put this in air quotes, remembering with a sting of shame how she'd rallied against this notion, thinking it would bore her to tears to have a professional job in the future. All she'd wanted when she was in her mid-teens was to have a family of her own and perhaps make a living in some sort of arty career.

How naïve she'd been.

'Well, why don't you have a think about what you'd feel comfortable telling people you do? You're a business owner; why don't you go with that?'

She nodded slowly, her earlier irritation at his imagined snobbery subsiding. 'Okay. Business owner it is.'

He nodded. 'And what do you intend to tell your family about our arrangement?' he asked in a careful tone.

'I'm going to say I've taken a job as your live-in housekeeper, for which you're going to pay me an exorbitant wage.'

He nodded, then pulled out his phone and began to type onto the touch screen, presumably making a note of her demands, and his, so they'd have something to refer back to should there be any issues in the future.

'They'd buy that much more readily than the truth – that I'm marrying a total stranger,' she added with a strange tingling feeling in her throat.

It felt so odd to say those words. Whenever she'd imagined getting married, which hadn't been very often recently, owing to her life being too complicated for her to think that far into the future, she'd imagined herself meeting a guy, their mutual love of board games bringing them together, and dating him for a couple of years before moving in together, then him proposing to her out of the blue in some far-flung romantic destination, like Hawaii or Morocco, or maybe on a Mediterranean island whilst sailing through the clear blue water on a yacht.

They'd get married in a quaint little church with all their friends and family watching and throw a huge party afterwards, where they'd dance the night away together. Then, a year or two later, after they'd had some time together as a couple, they'd have kids, maybe three or four of them.

She'd always wanted a big family.

When she was younger, sitting bored and frustrated at school during subjects she couldn't get a handle on no matter how hard she tried, she'd fantasised about what it would be like to be a mother. How she'd make her kids big bowls of hearty food, which they'd gobble down gratefully before going off to play happily with their toys, or do finger-painting with her at the kitchen table, laughing about the mess they were making together. Or she'd imagine ruffling their hair at the school gates and receiving rib-crushing hugs in return before they ran in, with her shouting that she loved them, which they'd pretend to find embarrassing but would secretly adore. Then later in the evening she'd tuck her sleepy, happy kids up into bed before spending the rest of the evening with her gorgeous husband, chatting about the day they'd had before retiring to bed together hand in hand.

That all seemed a million miles away now though.

It had been ages since she'd been on a proper date with anyone and even then, they'd barely got to the kissing stage before her lifestyle and responsibilities had got in the way of things developing any further. She'd made it clear that her family came first and that had destroyed the chances of a relationship.

Not that she blamed her mother and sister. Not a bit. In fact, despite their difficult circumstances, she quite liked being the head of the family. The one that everyone relied on. It gave her a sense of purpose that had previously been lacking in her life.

Yes, anyway, it was a good thing that Xavier had insisted on a purely platonic relationship. It wasn't like she had any time for romance.

'How old are you, Soli?' Xavier asked brusquely, jolting her back to the present.

A shiver of disquiet tickled down her spine. Was he worried she wasn't mature enough to deal with this?

'I'm twenty-one,' she said, setting back her shoulders and fixing him with a determined stare. 'Old enough to know my own mind,' she added firmly.

His eyes assessed her for a couple of beats more before he nodded. 'Okay, then. I guess that's everything we need to discuss today.' He put his phone down on his desk, arranging it so it sat parallel with his keyboard, before looking up and giving her his full attention again. 'Look, I appreciate this is a lot to take in right now, so why don't you go away and have a think about it, to make sure you're comfortable with everything we've discussed? It's a big decision to make and I don't expect you to sign up for it until you've had a chance to check me out first.'

She nodded jerkily. Despite her bravado, she was actually glad of the chance to go and think about this away from his discombobulating presence, just to make sure she hadn't overlooked something important. 'Okay. I'll do that. It really wouldn't do to marry an axe murderer by mistake,' she said, flashing him a jokey grin.

Ignoring her attempt at levity, he opened a drawer in his desk and took out a business card which he handed to her. 'This has my personal mobile number and address on it. Give me a call when you're ready to talk again.' He paused and frowned. 'But don't leave it too long or I might find someone else to marry in the meantime.'

For a second she wasn't sure whether he was joking or not. He didn't seem to do smiling, at least not the kind that made him look as though he was genuinely happy. Cynical. That was what he came across as. And reserved.

She wondered fleetingly what had happened to him to make him like that, but pushed the thought away. It wasn't important right now and she really shouldn't allow herself to get emotionally attached to him anyway, not if this was going to work as a purely business arrangement.

'Okay, thanks. I'll get in touch very soon,' she replied, taking the card from his fingers.

She shot him a tense smile, then got up from the desk on shaky legs and turned to go.

'And Solitaire.'

She turned back.

'If I find out the details of this proposition have been leaked to the press I'll know where to find you.' There was a heavy pause before he added, 'And you'll find your business and your family swiftly evicted from my property.'

'Understood,' she said, then left the office of her potential future husband, wondering what in the heck she'd just got herself into.

*   *   *

Back at the cafe, she relieved Callie, who waitressed for them a lot and had kindly agreed to work an extra shift that morning so Soli could go to the McQueen Property office. Once she'd caught up with the daily tasks and served a sudden rush of customers, she sat behind the serving counter with her laptop and typed Xavier's name into the search engine with trembling fingers.

She'd already looked him up before the meeting, of course, scouring the web pages for something she could use in her defence against him, but to her frustration had found him to be squeaky clean. At least at first glance. She needed to put in more thorough due diligence here though if she was going to commit to live with the man for a year. The last thing she needed was to find herself sucked into something she'd not anticipated and then couldn't escape from without causing more harm to her situation.

But as hard as she looked, she couldn't find anything that threw even the meanest of shadows over his reputation.

The only things that came up about him were on gossip sites, where they mentioned him in relation to the high-society women he'd had flings with over the last few years. The man appeared to be some kind of international playboy, always showing up at high-profile fundraisers and gallery openings with a different, instantly recognisable woman on his arm. He was like a character from one of the romantic novels she liked to gobble up like sweets for escapism from her busy, stressful existence. She'd never really believed such a person could exist in real life, but here he was, a living, breathing, alpha male business tycoon.

So he checked out okay online.

Picking up her phone, she called a friend who was a police officer in the Met and asked him if there was any way he could have a check around about Xavier, pretending she was doing it for business reasons concerning the cafe. Mercifully, her friend seemed to buy that and asked her to leave it with him.

She spent the rest of the day in a jumpy, nerve-filled state and was mightily relieved when her friend called her back in the early evening to let her know that nothing negative at all had come back to him with regard to Xavier, either personally or with his business. It seemed he was an upstanding citizen of the realm.

The only thing left to do now was to check out exactly where his house was using an online map app – just to make sure he wasn't expecting her to live in some kind of broken-down hovel. Not that she expected to encounter that. Judging by the high-end furniture and breathtaking elegance of his office, she couldn't imagine his house being a place she wouldn't like to spend time in. She could have happily lived right there in his office if he'd asked her to, with that wonderful view over the water. It certainly beat the one she had from their living room window over the busy, vehicle-choked high street, or the one of the bins in their small back yard from the bedroom she shared with her sister.

Not that she was complaining about her lot. Home was where her family was, and she'd been happy living here above the cafe with them. Staying in this flat had made her feel closer to her father somehow. She could still picture him sitting in the battered old leather armchair by the window after long shifts in the cafe, with a paperback resting on his knee and his requisite triple-shot black coffee on the small table beside him. He'd hated working at the bank so after twenty years he'd finally given up corporate life and they'd all downsized so he could run the board game cafe, a dream he'd had for years.

Sadly, he'd only worked there for five years before he died. Still, Soli was glad he'd had the opportunity to realise his dream. Ever since she'd lost him, the cafe had become a symbol of hope for her, as well as a reminder that hard work and dedication paid off – something she'd been slow to learn in her younger years, to her everlasting shame.

Shaking off the guilt that always gave her a painful jab when she remembered how selfishly she'd acted in her teens, she got up from behind the counter to close up after the last stragglers made their way out onto the street, waving cheerily to her and calling their thanks. If only they had more regulars like them, the type that bought food and drink every hour as they played, the cafe would have some hope of survival.

She just needed to find a way to entice those types of people to walk through the door.

After locking up behind them and giving the floor a sweep and the tables one last wipe, Soli walked into the middle of the room and tried to survey it with objective eyes. Why weren't people coming in as much as they'd used to? Sure, it was a bit shabby looking now after years of wear and tear and it could probably do with a bit of sprucing up, but it had a friendly, comfortable aura to it, and didn't people love shabby chic these days?

She hated the idea of messing with what her father had done to the cafe. He'd sanded and varnished the wooden tables himself, painted the walls, chosen the now slightly chipped crockery, and she couldn't imagine any of it changing. It would be like wiping her father's soul from the place.

She shuddered, hating the very thought of that.

No, she'd try advertising first, then think about any alterations they might have to make once the money was flowing in again.

Assuming they didn't lose the tenancy in the meantime.

Taking a breath, she focused on calming her suddenly raging pulse. All she needed to do was marry Xavier McQueen and everything would be okay.

The utter bizarreness of that thought made her laugh out loud.

Shaking her head at the surreal turn her life had taken, she picked up her phone and tapped in the number he'd given her.

He picked up after two rings.

'Xavier McQueen.'

'It's Soli.'

'Hi,' was all he said in reply.

There was a pause in which the weight of expectation hung heavily in the air.

'So, I checked up on you and it turns out you're not an axe murderer,' she quipped nervously.

There was an uncomfortable pause when he didn't respond.

Okay, then. Jokes weren't deemed appropriate right now. Wow, this guy was so business-like.

Probably best just to get down to business, then.

'So, I've thought about it, and I still want to go ahead with our deal.'

'Great, that's great.' She could hear the relief in his voice. 'I'll arrange for a solicitor to draw up a prenuptial contract and another one that states the terms of our deal, which we'll both need to sign.' His tone was professional again now.

'I'll give notice at the register office that we want to get married, but we'll have to wait twenty-eight days before we can legally perform the ceremony. The closest one is near St Pancras Station, but I'm assuming you won't have an issue with where the formality of it takes place.' It wasn't a question, she realised. 'It's not like we'll be having a big celebration with friends and family,' he added when she didn't reply right away.

'Er, no, that's fine.' The words came out sounding confident, but something deep in her chest did a strange, sickening sort of flip. This really wasn't the way she'd imagined it happening – getting married – but, as he'd rightly pointed out, this wasn't meant to be a romantic event, it was a business transaction and should be treated as such. There was no room for any kind of emotional attachment. She'd make sure her real wedding, to the guy who loved and cherished her, was a big, exciting affair, with all her friends and family present. That one would be a cause for a true celebration. She just needed to keep that in mind when she signed the register. True love would come later in her life, when she finally had the time and energy to consider it a possibility.

'Okay, good. I'll let you know the details as soon as I've set it up. I'll need some personal documents from you which I'll swing by and pick up tomorrow, if that works for you?'

'N-no problem,' she stuttered, feeling suddenly as though her life was running away from her a little.

It's not surprising; you're getting married in a month.

A shiver of nerves tickled down her spine.

There was a lot to sort out before then, not least accepting the university place for Domino and finding a full-time carer for her mum, as well as giving notice at the gastropub and hiring someone to cover her shifts at the cafe.

The mere thought of all the work and organisation ahead of her was exhausting.

This is for the family, she reminded herself as panic threatened to engulf her. *And it's only temporary.*

In a year's time her life would have taken on a whole new shape. She was doing this for all the right reasons and once she and Xavier were divorced, she'd be free to fall in love and get married for real.

With that thought in mind, she told Xavier goodbye and hung up.

Trying to ignore the now almost overwhelming wave of nerves, she turned off all the lights in the cafe, hid a yawn behind her hand and trudged up the narrow staircase to the flat, first to check that her mother didn't need anything, then to spend the next hour or so planning how best to kick-start the beginning of her brand-new life.

3

SCRABBLE – CHOOSE YOUR WORDS CAREFULLY.

Their wedding day was glorious. At least the weather was, with the sun pouring in on them through the large picture windows of the register office as they stood at the desk reciting the lines they were asked to say.

The huge room, with its rows of chairs facing the desk, was eerily empty except for Xavier and Soli, the registrar, Xavier's friend, Russell – the only friend he'd confided in and who had drawn up the contracts in his other role as a solicitor – and one other witness, who was a complete stranger to them all. Xavier had approached him outside on the street, pretending that their second witness had been delayed in traffic, and offered him a wad of cash for half an hour of his time.

Glancing around the room, he remembered all too well the last time he'd been in a place like this as echoes of a clawing sense of shame and dread pricked at his skin. He'd promised himself he'd never set foot in a register office again and hadn't attended a wedding since his own disastrous debacle. He'd actually intended to avoid them for the rest of his life, if at all possible.

But he hadn't counted on his Aunt Faith's iron-like will.

So here he was again.

At least this time the bride had turned up and actually married him.

Well, you got what you wanted, Aunty. I hope you're happy now.

Soli, to her credit, didn't say a thing about the lack of guests or the stranger signing the marriage register beneath her name. In fact, she'd seemed more than happy to let him deal with all the arrangements and go along with what-ever he'd asked her to do. She'd told him it had meant she'd been able to focus fully on making the necessary arrangements for her family and the cafe before she came to live with him. Apparently, her sister was off to Oxford over the summer to earn some extra "unexpected expenses" cash at a live-in job she'd found there before her first year began and her mother now had a full-time carer staying in the flat with her. All thanks to his money.

Not that he resented it. It meant he was able to achieve exactly what he wanted, after all.

In his experience, money always smoothed the way. It was the only thing he could ever really rely on.

'Congratulations,' the registrar said to the two of them once the ceremony had come to a close. She didn't seem at all fazed by the lack of guests or the sombreness of the occasion, but Xavier guessed she must have seen it all in the course of her duties.

'Thank you,' he said, giving her a nod of gratitude.

'Yes, it was a lovely service,' Soli added with a barely discernible quaver in her voice.

He glanced at her, wondering whether she was having a moment of regret, but she just smiled back at him as if nothing in the world was wrong. He appre-ciated her professionalism.

He'd not really looked at what she was wearing when they'd met in the lobby only minutes before their slot because the registrar had come straight over to introduce herself then whisked them straight in, but as he surveyed Soli now he realised she'd made a real effort with her appearance today.

Her wild curls had been tamed into an elegant up do and she'd put on more make-up than he'd previously seen her wear, which accentuated her big bright eyes and full, rosebud mouth.

The simple cream-coloured sheath dress she wore exposed her slim, toned arms and flowed over her curves, drawing his gaze to the tantalising swell of her breasts under the thin fabric.

Hoping she'd assume he was looking at the small posy of flowers she clutched in front of her, he cleared his throat and raised his eyes to give her a tight smile.

Yes, she definitely looked the part. She was a very attractive woman and no one would find it strange that he'd chosen to marry her. At least on the surface.

As long as she kept her mouth shut about the terms of the deal they'd worked out, his secret would be safe.

Hopefully there wouldn't be many opportunities for their charade to be discovered anyway. He'd asked her to be ready to attend functions with him, but he wasn't actually intending to take her along to many. Just one or two, so it didn't look odd if anyone checked up on them.

He'd already alerted his great-aunt's solicitor to the fact he was getting married and had been told to expect spot checks in the next few months, just to satisfy her conditions. After a year the title deeds to the house would pass into his name.

Then he'd be free to live his life as he chose again.

One year wasn't too long a time to maintain this farce. He could manage it.

'Well, Mrs McQueen, now that's over, shall we get out of here?' he suggested once the registrar had departed, more than ready to leave the place now.

To his surprise Soli pressed her lips together and pulled a mock horrified face. 'You know, I thought Solitaire Saunders was bad, but Solitaire McQueen?' She raised both eyebrows. 'My father will be dancing with glee in his grave.'

The sad edge to her voice gave him pause. 'How did your father die? If you don't mind me asking?'

She shrugged. 'I don't mind. I guess you should know now that we're husband and wife.' Taking a breath, she pushed her shoulders back a little, as if using the action to give her courage. 'He was knocked off his bike by a guy who was texting whilst driving. He died instantly.'

A prickle of horror rushed up Xavier's spine. 'Ah, hell, that's awful. I'm so sorry.'

There was an awkward pause while she blinked back the tears that had pooled in her eyes.

'Thank you,' she whispered, smiling bravely. 'I still miss him every day, but he'd want to know we were all getting on with our lives without him.' She glanced down at the slim white gold ring he'd placed on her finger only minutes ago with an expression of incredulity on her face, then flashed him a wry smile. 'I'm not sure what he'd think about me marrying a stranger though.'

'I'm sure he'd approve if he knew you were doing it for the right reasons,' Xavier pointed out.

Nodding, she let out a small chuckle. 'Yeah, I'd like to think so. He always said I'd get myself in a knotty situation one day with my impulsiveness, but I don't think this was quite the scenario he had in mind.'

Her cheeks had flushed an attractive shade of pink, and he had the strangest urge to stroke his fingers across her skin and feel the heat he knew must be there.

Don't be a fool, McQueen.

Instead he nodded jerkily in response to her joke, then gestured towards the exit. 'Well, anyway, we should leave the room before the next wedding party arrives,' he said stiffly, wishing he didn't sound like such an uptight prig.

Giving her body a small jiggle, as if shaking off her melancholy, Soli nodded in agreement.

He marched ahead of her, trying to blank his mind of the way her voluptuous body had shimmied in his vision, as he held the door open for her.

A hubbub of noise surrounded them as they entered the lobby and walked through a large group of people that had gathered there, presumably to attend the next marriage that was taking place in the room they'd just vacated.

Russell and the other witness appeared beside them as they made their way towards the exit. Xavier hadn't noticed them slipping out while they were talking to the registrar, but he suspected Russell had suggested they made themselves scarce so he wouldn't find himself having to answer any awkward questions.

'Let's go out to the front of the building and I'll take a couple of photos of you both in your wedding gear, then we'll see if we can grab a passer-by to take one with the four of us in it,' Russell murmured into his ear.

'Good idea,' Xavier agreed, heading towards the large doors at the other side of the vestibule.

Once outside, they posed next to the register office sign while Russell fiddled with his XLR camera, which he stood on a tripod. Once it was set up, he directed them to stand closer together, with Xavier's arm around Soli's waist and her body pressed close to his. They shuffled awkwardly into the pose and Russell had just taken the first photo when a loud and uncomfortably familiar voice boomed out behind them.

'McQueen? Is that you, old boy?'

Turning reluctantly, with his heart in his mouth, Xavier came face to face with the one person he really could have done without bumping into today.

'Hugo. Good to see you. What brings you here today?' he said, letting go of

Soli and taking a deliberate step in front of her so she was obscured from Hugo's line of sight as he shook the man's hand.

'A colleague's getting married, and I promised to attend.' He leaned towards Xavier conspiratorially and cocked an eyebrow. 'He's on track to become my boss one day soon so I thought I'd do the smart thing and turn up today. Show willing, you know?'

'Sure. I hear you,' Xavier said. He knew exactly how these old boy networks worked. It wasn't wise to snub someone who had the potential to either super-charge your career or ruin it for you in the future.

'Is Veronica with you?' Xavier asked, a little panicked at the thought of having to save face in front of Hugo's scarily perceptive wife as well.

'No, she's off on some girls' retreat, lucky mare!' he said loudly, adding in a jovial guffaw for good measure. It seemed Xavier's attempt to hide Soli hadn't been successful, though, because Hugo leaned to one side to peer past him. 'And who is this, may I ask?'

Xavier swallowed down his exasperation. 'This is Soli.'

She took a step forwards and held out her hand, giving Hugo a warm smile. 'Solitaire McQueen,' she said, as if happy to have the opportunity to test out her new name for the first time.

Bad timing, Soli. Very bad.

Not that she could have known that.

'McQueen, you say?' Hugo boomed, giving Xavier a confused glance, then looking towards where Russell stood with the camera. 'Have the two of you—' he waggled a finger between them '—just got married?'

'Yes, just a few minutes ago,' Soli confirmed, to Xavier's chagrin.

'Well. You are a dark horse, McQueen. We had no idea marriage was on the cards for you.' Hugo's confused frown deepened as he looked between the two of them.

'No, well, it all happened very quickly,' Xavier said, his heart sinking through his chest. 'We've dated on and off for years but only recently decided we should make a proper go of it,' he lied, silently begging his friend to take him at his word.

'Really?' Hugo said with a tinge of disbelief in his voice. 'It happened so quickly you couldn't even wait to invite your friends to the wedding?'

Damn. He was well and truly busted. He'd never hear the end of it from his old friends now.

'Neither of us wanted a big do,' Xavier said gruffly, feeling heat rise up his throat. The last thing he needed was Hugo and his old social group to find out he'd had to pay Soli to marry him in order to keep his family home. He hated the idea of that getting back to Harriet. His humiliation really would be complete then.

'We thought we'd have a party for close friends and family some time in the near future,' he said, deciding the only thing to do was to bluster his way through this.

Hugo flashed him a knowing smile. 'Fair enough, old chap. I suppose I can understand why you'd choose not to shout about it to all and sundry.' Turning away before Xavier could comment on that, he asked, 'And what do you do, Soli?'

He noticed her shoulders stiffen at the question and silently prayed she'd be able to handle this unexpected confrontation without making Hugo suspicious about the real state of their relationship. 'I'm a small-business owner in the catering industry and one of Xavier's clients,' she said, somewhat mechanically.

Xavier cringed at how that must have sounded to Hugo, but mercifully he didn't seem to find anything odd about it.

'Well, I must congratulate you, Soli; I never thought I'd see a woman manage to make an honest man of Xavier McQueen,' he said, aiming a cheerful grin in her direction. 'Any particular reason for getting married right now though? Do we have the patter of tiny McQueen feet to look forward to?' Hugo asked with a sly wink.

'No,' Xavier stated coldly, feeling the atmosphere thicken between them. 'It just felt like the right time for us both,' he added, trying to smooth over the extremity of his reaction.

Hugo didn't take offence though and slapped him hard on the arm. 'Sorry, old chap, didn't mean to put my foot in it. The wife's always telling me off for that! Very happy for you both, obviously. I'll have to tell Veronica I saw you; she'll be delighted.'

He felt Soli look round at him but didn't turn his head.

'In fact,' his friend went on, completely oblivious to the discomfort he was inflicting, 'if you're not going on honeymoon right away...' He paused and looked at them expectantly.

The only thing they could do was shake their heads dumbly, caught out by the question.

'Well, in that case, why don't the two of you come over to our place next weekend? We're having a bit of a do to celebrate our fifth wedding anniversary – all Veronica's idea, you know,' he added with a pseudo grimace towards Soli. 'I know she'd be delighted to see you, McQueen, and to meet you too, Soli.'

'I'm not sure—' Xavier began to argue.

'Don't be a bore, McQueen!' Hugo broke in before Xavier had chance to air an excuse. 'You can't hide from us forever. And Veronica will never forgive you if you don't accept at least one of our social invitations. We've not seen hide nor hair of you for years! Now you're married you've no excuse not to come along to see the old crowd. You don't want folks thinking you're shunning them, now, do you?' he said this with a laugh in his voice, but Xavier knew it covered a real sense of hurt. Clearly Hugo was nursing a sense of resentment about being ignored and avoided for so long.

He was trapped. Damned if he did and damned if he didn't.

They'd have a week to prepare for it though. That ought to be enough time for him and Soli to get to know each other well enough to convince Hugo and Veronica, and anyone else they'd invited, that they were a real, loving couple.

'I'm pretty sure we're free then,' he conceded. 'We'll check our diaries and let you know.'

'Great! I'll get Veronica to send you an official invite,' Hugo said with affable gumption. 'You still in your aunt's Hampstead pad?'

'Yes. I'm still there,' Xavier said, feeling a desperate urge to get away from his friend now so he could regain his shaky composure. 'I look forward to receiving the invite, Hugo. Anyway, we'd better get on. We need to take a couple more photos, then we have some celebrating to do,' he added in an upbeat voice that didn't sound like his own, forcing himself to give Hugo a happy-looking smile.

'You've picked a real charmer there, Soli,' Hugo said with another wink in her direction. 'I hope he's intending to treat you like a princess today.'

'Oh, I fully expect him to,' Soli replied, smiling back. 'He's the most generous man I've ever met.'

Xavier experienced a rush of gratitude towards her for that.

'I tell you what, Hugo,' Xavier said, as a flash of inspiration struck him. 'Since you're here, let's have you in the photo too. It'll only take two seconds. We just need to grab someone to press the button for us – it's all set up.'

'Sure! Be happy to!' Hugo boomed, clearly pleased to be included. 'This lovely lady will do it for us, won't you?' he said, making a large beckoning motion to a woman in a big red hat who was just about to enter the doors of the register office.

'Er... yes, of course,' she said, looking over at first Xavier, then Soli, and giving them a warm, indulgent smile.

So they all bunched together and the lady took a couple of pictures of the five of them.

'Thanks so much,' Xavier said, pleased with his quick thinking. It would look much better to have at least two of his friends in the wedding photos.

'We should do one more of just you and Soli, for safety,' Russell said to Xavier, before they all dispersed.

'Ooh, yes. You make such a gorgeous couple,' the woman said, beaming at the two of them. 'You should do one with the two of you kissing. I always think they're the nicest ones to have displayed.'

There was a small pause where neither of them reacted.

'Er... yes, good idea,' Soli said a little too loudly beside him and he felt her slip her arm around his back and lean in towards him, giving him a slightly awkward cuddle.

For a moment he stiffened under her touch before realising how odd that would seem to the small group that were looking at them intently now.

Without allowing himself to think about it, he slid his hand against her jaw, tipped her head towards him and kissed her fully on the mouth.

She drew in a small, breathy gasp, but didn't pull away, instead sinking into the kiss and wrapping her arms tightly around his waist as he instinctively opened his mouth against hers. The soft, flowery scent of her enveloped his senses and he breathed her in deeply, struck by the distinctiveness of her taste and smell.

Delicious.

Her lips were so soft and perfectly pliant he experienced the strangest sensation that they were somehow made to perfectly fit with his. His stomach swooped at the thought and he became aware of something deep inside him – long buried – beginning to stir.

Sensation fizzed along his veins, causing his breath to shorten and his heart to pound against his chest.

Oh Lord, that's not good.

Pulling abruptly away, he didn't dare look her in the eye again in case she saw even a hint of the heavy need that now pulsed through him. 'Was that okay? Did you get it?' he asked Russell, who was standing behind the camera looking at the two of them with an odd expression on his face.

'Yes, perfect. I got it,' his friend replied, quickly rearranging his features into a smile.

Xavier's stomach twisted as he realised that the spark he'd felt between them had outwardly showed. Not that that was necessarily a bad thing. At least to Hugo it would have looked as though they were genuinely attracted to each other.

When he glanced back at Soli he noticed she looked as bewildered as he felt, and his stomach knotted even tighter.

'Well, I'd better get inside before I miss the beginning of this thing,' Hugo said loudly, strolling over to give Xavier a slap on the back and jolting him out of his tangled thoughts. 'Looking forward to seeing the two of you next weekend.' And with that he gave them both a farewell salute and strode quickly away.

Xavier swallowed, his mouth suddenly dry and his head tight around the temples.

'I'd better go too!' the lady in the red hat said, glancing at her watch and moving towards the door of the register office. 'Congratulations, you two, and good luck for the future!'

Luck? Yes, they might need a bit of that if this fake marriage was going to go without a hitch.

'I guess we'd better get on, then,' he said, pulling himself together and turning to look at Soli.

'Okay. Sure. Great,' she replied, her expression still a little shell-shocked. Something tugged hard inside him as a strangely protective instinct appeared from nowhere.

He shook it off.

He needed to get on top of this weird, edgy feeling that was messing with his head. It was this place, it had to be; it was bringing back too many long-suppressed emotions. He couldn't allow himself to develop any kind of feelings for Soli, or encourage her to have any for him. It could cause all sorts of problems.

And extra problems were something neither of them needed right now.

4

SNAKES & LADDERS – A FRUSTRATING GAME OF UPS AND DOWNS.

Soli stood in front of the register office, having just kissed her new husband for the very first time, trying to deal with a strange sort of unease at finding she'd enjoyed it much more than was probably healthy for a woman who was now expected to live a life of celibacy for the next twelve months.

How had it been possible to feel so much in so few seconds?

She'd thought it would be fine, kissing Xavier for the camera with everyone looking on, but she'd been shocked by how her body had responded to him. Her skin had flushed all over as if the sun had concentrated all its power on her in those moments and her heart had done a triple flip before sinking to somewhere in the region of her stomach.

It had been wonderful and terrible all at the same time.

She wished she hadn't liked it quite so much because she now had a year to think about how wonderful Xavier's mouth felt on hers without being allowed to experience it again. He'd made it very clear this relationship wasn't ever going to be anything more than just friends.

Friends. But were they really? Could they be?

'I'll go and get your bags from the cloakroom,' Xavier said brusquely.

All she could do was nod in agreement, then watch him stride back into the building where she'd stashed the two cases she'd packed so carefully the day before. They represented the sum total of her worldly goods, apart from a few items of clothing she'd given to Domino, and a small box of mementoes from her childhood which she'd left back at the flat because she'd not wanted to lug them over to his house.

Taking a moment to compose herself while Xavier wasn't around, she took a breath and pushed back her shoulders, uncomfortably aware that her legs were still wobbling like mad after she'd put herself through the most nerve-racking half-hour of her life – first the actual marriage ceremony, during which she'd felt as though she were looking down on herself from above, then the whole surreal exchange when Xavier's friend Hugo had appeared out of nowhere and she'd had to scrabble for the correct way to act in front of him.

In the heat of the moment, she'd just gone for it and introduced herself as Solitaire McQueen without considering that this might not be something Xavier would approve of, but she'd realised from the way he'd stiffened, then scowled at her, that it had been a mistake. But then, how was she supposed to have known how he wanted her to act in front of his acquaintances? They'd been so busy sorting out the legal side of things they hadn't got round to discussing the day-to-day business of being married yet. It had all been such a whirl.

She'd tried hard not to take offence at his obvious reluctance to introduce her to his friend, but it still rankled. Obviously Xavier wouldn't want the marriage of convenience part to be public knowledge, she understood that – he was clearly a private and proud man and if people found out the amounts of money he'd promised to pay her to go through with it neither of them would come out looking particularly good – but surely he wasn't planning on not telling his friends that he was married to her.

Judging by Hugo's reaction it sounded as though Xavier had kept the marriage a secret from all of his friends too, apart from Russell, of course, who had written up the legal documents for them to sign and so was clearly a necessary confidant.

She turned to look at Russell now, who was standing quietly beside her, and wondered what he thought about the whole strange undertaking.

He must have felt her gaze on him because he turned to look at her and asked, 'How well do you know Xavier?' as if he'd been wondering the same things that she had. From his expression she suspected he was actually a bit concerned about what his friend had just done.

'Uh, hardly at all,' she said with a pained grimace. 'We've not spent a lot of time together because we've been too busy sorting out our personal situations before the ceremony. It's all been a bit of a whirlwind to be honest.'

Russell nodded thoughtfully, then gave her an encouraging smile. 'Listen, I know he comes across as a bit distant sometimes, but he's a good guy. He's just been through a lot during his life, that's all, and it's made him a bit hard to reach. Emotionally, I mean.'

'Really? What happened?' Soli asked, intrigued by what Russell might have to tell her. If Xavier was going to keep her at a distance, talking to his friends would probably be the only way to really get to know more about him.

Russell looked uncomfortable. 'I should probably let him tell you all that himself. It's not really my place.' He rocked back onto his heels and crossed his arms. 'You've got a year to get him to lower his barriers, after all,' he said, his smile a little strained now. 'I'll just say this—' he paused, as if searching for the right words to use '—you should keep in mind that he's unlikely to want to commit to the marriage fully. What I mean is, don't get your hopes up that he'll let it become a real relationship. I don't think he's really cut out for that sort of commitment. Not any more.'

Soli nodded, but couldn't help but frown, feeling a bit overwhelmed by it all now. 'Don't worry, I'm not looking for it to turn into a real marriage either,' she said assertively, though something in the back of her mind let out a small squeak of protest.

No. She'd be a fool to even consider that happening. She was only doing this for the year, then she'd be in a much better position to commit her heart for real. With someone who truly cared about her.

The momentousness of what she'd just done suddenly hit her full force, sucking her breath away.

She was married and about to move in with a man she barely knew.

Adrenaline surged through her body, making her hands shake.

'A year suddenly feels like an awfully long time to live with a stranger,' she blurted.

Russell gave her a reassuring smile. 'Don't worry, he'll look after you. He's nothing if not a gentleman.'

Xavier reappeared through the doors with her bags then and came over to thank Russell for his help, giving him a friendly slap on the back, before turning to face her.

'Are you ready to go home?'

Home.

His home though, not hers.

'Yes, I'm ready when you are,' she said, summoning a smile, which she hoped wouldn't give away how nervous she was.

Xavier nodded, not seeming to notice her jitters, and set off at a brisk pace with her bags to where he'd left his car. He loaded her cases into the boot while she slipped into the passenger seat.

The car smelt wonderful: of new leather and Xavier's distinctive scent, a mixture of the aftershave he wore and a musky, masculine fragrance all of his own. She'd been hyper-aware of it in his office when she'd first met him and it had haunted her ever since, the olfactory memory appearing in the air at random moments, though she'd known she was only imagining it. Her mind was good at playing tricks on her like that. It had done the same thing after her father died, conjuring his scent at odd moments, bringing with it a surge of such painful grief she'd often been immobilised by it.

But this definitely wasn't a time for immobility. She needed to make good on this opportunity and she was determined to do everything in her power to make this deal work out well – for both of them.

Sensing Xavier needed a few minutes to process what had just happened too, Soli stayed quiet as they pulled away from the kerb and stared out of the window, watching the busy London streets slip by.

When he still hadn't said a word to her as they began to drive through Hampstead Village towards the road where he lived – where they lived – she found she couldn't stand the silence any longer. Turning to look at him, she experienced a wave of concern when she caught sight of his rigid profile.

'Is everything okay?' she asked quietly. 'I'm sorry if I did something wrong back there. I thought Hugo was a friend of yours so it'd be okay to introduce myself. Surely you weren't hoping to keep me a secret for the next year...' Pausing, she took a shaky breath. 'Were you?' She laughed nervously, concern creeping over her skin as she considered the possibility that she'd hit upon the correct answer.

'No, no, of course not, it's fine,' he said, but his tone wasn't exactly convincing. 'I hadn't really thought about how I'd handle telling people about us, so it caught me off guard, that's all. But I think he bought the whirlwind marriage thing.' He turned to look at her now and his set expression softened a little. 'No point dwelling on it though. It's done.'

'No. Okay.' His answer hadn't done much to calm her nerves, but she decided to push her concern to the back of her mind. He was right – there was no point worrying about it. She'd figure him out eventually.

They'd need to spend some quality time together this week if they were going to look like a convincing couple at Hugo's party next weekend though. The last thing she wanted was to put her foot in it again with his friends. She hated the idea of making a fool of herself in front of them. If she and Xavier weren't careful something like that could potentially cause resentment and tension between them, which would make for a really uncomfortable home life. She really didn't want that. Not if they were going to have to live with each other for the next year.

After driving along the long, wide road locally referred to as 'Millionaire's Row', she'd expected Xavier's house to be impressive, but as they swung in through the automatic gates at the end of the driveway, which magically opened for his car, the true magnificence of the place struck her like a blow to the stomach. Built in the arts and crafts style, it loomed above her like an enormous geometric citadel, its two wings standing like sentries either side of the grand entrance.

'Home, sweet home,' he said, turning momentarily to raise both eyebrows at her as he pulled the car up to the front of the house, then turned off the engine. 'I'll grab your cases, then I'll show you around.'

Taking a moment to get another swell of nerves under control, she watched him get out of the car and take her bags out of the boot, then dragged in a deep, steadying breath and got out too, following him to the front door, which he was opening with a swipe card.

It was like walking into another world as Soli took her first step into the house, letting out a gasp of wonder.

'You weren't expecting me to carry you over the threshold, were you?' Xavier asked gruffly, possibly mistaking her stunned awe for upset as she stood there, gazing around the cavernous, marble-floored entrance hall with wide eyes.

'No, of course not,' she said, giving him a reassuring smile before returning her gaze to the dark wooden banister staircase, which drew the eye upwards towards an ornate mullioned window, its many panes of glass winking in the late-afternoon sunshine. Looking at it, she wouldn't be surprised to find this one room had the same square footage as her entire cafe.

'Wow. I can see why you wouldn't want to lose this place. It's spectacular!' she said, turning to flash him an impressed look.

He glanced around him as if checking out what she meant, then gave her a taut smile back.

'It's been in my family for nearly a hundred and fifty years, but I've only had the privilege of living here for the last four – since my great-aunt was taken into hospital after her first stroke.'

'That must have been hard. Coming to live here on your own when she was so ill.'

He shrugged but didn't say anything. There was a glimmer of sadness in his eyes though, she was sure of it.

'Have you done much to it?' she asked, sensing his intention to keep the subject on a non-emotional level.

'Hardly a thing, which was great for me because I could just move straight in.' He gesticulated around the large, elegant entrance hall with its neat marble-topped table and large vase of fresh flowers sitting invitingly in the middle of the space. The subtly coloured walls were hung with striking pieces of modern art, and there was a huge gilt-framed mirror on the far one which reflected their images back to them.

'She had really good taste and a love of interior design, so kept up with all the trends. She was always poring over those house and garden magazines,' he said with a faraway look in his eyes, as if remembering her fondly. 'I'm sure she would have been an interior designer if she'd had the chance, but my great-uncle didn't want her to work. He was pretty traditional like that.'

'Right. Wow.' She couldn't imagine a world in which she wouldn't be allowed to work. She'd be bored to tears.

'Let me give you the tour,' he said, already moving towards one of the large mahogany doors that stood open to the right of them.

He guided her around the frankly massive ground floor: through the sitting room with its classy antique furniture, the library with its shelves stuffed with old books, the snug with a huge widescreen TV on the wall and a squashy-looking sofa facing it, and then on to what he called the morning room, which looked as though no one ever used it. She guessed the William Morris wallpaper in there was original, due to its slightly faded look.

She couldn't help but watch Xavier closely as he walked through the rooms ahead of her, his broad back straight and his long-legged gait a little tense. He intrigued her. Why was such an attractive, successful man living here alone? Maybe it had something to do with the not-believing-in-love thing.

Best not to think about that, though. She didn't want to get herself in any kind of emotional tangle. She had enough to deal with right now.

He then led her towards the back of the house, where there was a fully equipped gym, and on through another frosted glass door leading to an indoor swimming pool, which was surrounded by green-leafed plants in pots standing against the beautiful mosaic-tiled walls.

'You can use this any time you like,' he said, waving his hand at it as if everyone had one and it wasn't anything special.

A little bubble of nervous excitement, that had begun to form in the pit of her stomach as soon as she'd entered the house, rose up to her throat and tickled her tongue.

This incredible place was going to be her home for the next year.

They ended the tour of the main house in a huge kitchen diner, which was the most well-worn looking place in the house. Even so, she guessed the oak kitchen cabinets and marble-topped work surfaces would have cost a pretty penny.

This room was clearly the heart of the home and Soli immediately felt much more relaxed in here. The rest of the house was beautiful, but it had been a bit like being shown around a stately home where you weren't allowed to touch anything.

She could imagine spending lots of time in this room though, making meals for them both and perhaps baking her locally famous cakes and biscuits for Xavier to sample. She'd welcome the chance to impress him with her cooking skills. It would make her feel less insignificant in the face of his overwhelming prowess.

He'd leant back against a scrubbed oak table in the middle of the tiled floor as she looked around, and she glanced over at him, wondering how many times he'd sat there to eat in his lifetime. She could imagine him as a bright-eyed, but serious, little boy with a wicked grin, when he chose to deploy it. Not that she'd seen any evidence of it so far. Any smiles he'd given her had seemed perfunctory and lacking in any real emotion.

What must he have gone through to not have any warmth in his smile? The thought of it made her inordinately sad, especially when it occurred to her that he might well have lost his spirit when he was a little boy.

But perhaps that wasn't the case. He seemed to have genuine love and affection for his great-aunt and clearly adored living here judging by the reverent tone he'd used when showing the rooms to her.

'Did your great-aunt have any children?' she asked, thinking what a wonderful house this would be for games of hide and seek. You could probably go for hours without being discovered with all the nooks and crannies available.

'No. I think she wanted them, but it never happened. My great-uncle died before I was born so I never met him, but I used to spend a lot of time with Aunt Faith and I think she considered me the child she never had. She always invited me here during my holidays from boarding school.'

'And your parents were okay with that? Didn't they want you at home with them?'

He let out a low snort. 'They didn't mind at all. They're not exactly "kid people".'

'Oh.' The sharp edge of tension in his voice disturbed her. Was he telling her that his parents didn't want anything to do with him? How heartbreaking.

'Anyway,' Xavier said loudly, making her jump, 'let me show you the room you'll be staying in. Part of the ground floor was converted into a bedroom for my great-aunt to live in, but wasn't used because she had the second stroke before she could move into it.'

She followed him out of the kitchen and back to the entrance hall, suspecting there would probably be a lot of Xavier suddenly changing the subject when things started to get too personal for his liking – which would be frustrating, considering she needed to get to know this enigmatic man a lot better in a very short space of time if they were going to come across as a convincing couple.

'It's down here,' he said, guiding her along a hallway towards the back of the house, then through a door with its own mortice lock and into a large, airy bedroom.

So, her bedroom was to be downstairs? As far away from Xavier's as possible, perhaps. Not that she had any right to question this. It was his home after all and she was, to all intents and purposes, his guest.

Like the kitchen in the main house, the bedroom was decorated in a warm, homey style, which immediately made her feel comfortable. There was a queen-sized bed against the wall on the far side and the rest of the room was kitted out in tasteful modern furniture, which, she suspected from its pristine gleam, had never been used before. Her heart fluttered as she realised there was a walk-in wardrobe. She'd only ever had half a small wardrobe at home, where she'd shared a room with Domino.

'You'll need to put some of your things, like toiletries and clothes, in my room too, just in case one of the solicitor's people drops round without giving us any notice and goes snooping. We don't want to give ourselves away by over-looking details like that,' Xavier said, crossing his arms, making him seem even more intimidating than usual.

The thought of being caught out like that only increased Soli's anxiety about them not knowing each other well enough yet. What if she had to answer questions about him that she didn't know the answers to? He could potentially lose his inheritance if the solicitor didn't believe they were a real couple, which would mean their deal would fall through and that could signal the end of the cafe.

'I can't lose this place, Soli, and I'm definitely not going to let it go to my money-grubbing cousin because we messed up the small stuff,' Xavier said, echoing her thoughts.

'Okay. No problem,' she said, trying to sound reassuring. She'd do every-thing in her power not to let that happen.

'Good. Well, now you've had a look around I'll bring your cases in here and you can get settled in.'

Following him out of the bedroom and back to the grand entrance hall, she tried not to let a feeling of being on the very edge of control overwhelm her.

She needed to focus on the positives, such as this amazing place being her home for the next year.

It would be so exciting to be here.

Or terrifying – depending on which way you chose to look at it.

Xavier seemed like a good guy though, if a little cold and reserved. Every-thing she'd found out about him had been positive, she reminded herself. Espe-cially the things she'd read about his business practices. And her father wouldn't have rented a property from a shyster after all; he'd always been a very cautious and thorough businessman himself.

'Why did your great-aunt want you to be married in order to inherit this place?' she blurted as they reached the front door. It had been playing on her mind as he'd shown her around. 'It seems a little extreme in this day and age.'

He turned back to face her with a grimace. 'Yes, well, my great-aunt had very traditional values. Her marriage was arranged by her family and she stayed married to my great-uncle for forty-three years, until he died of a heart attack. I think she had some romantic notion that if she forced me into getting married, I'd end up the same way she did. Blissfully happy.' He pulled a face.

'Not convinced, huh?'

'Not one bit.'

'Shame.'

He frowned. 'What do you mean?' From his tone she suspected he was unnerved to hear her talking about marriage in such a positive way. Perhaps because he was worried she might become more attached to the idea of being his wife than he was comfortable with.

'Don't worry,' she reassured him quickly. 'You're really not my type. When I get married for real it'll be because I'm in love with my partner and I want to spend the rest of my life with him. That won't happen with us.'

He continued to look at her in that unnervingly intense way he had, as if he was trying to read her innermost thoughts and catch sight of any lies she might be telling him. She stared boldly back, trying not to think about how devastatingly attractive he was.

'I promise you, I will not want to stay married to you after the year is up,' she reiterated firmly. 'I've got too much going on in my life to be a wife and mother right now.'

She was sure she saw him flinch when she said that, but before she could say anything more he nodded curtly and said, 'Anyway, you'll need these for the doors.' He pulled a plastic key card and a key for her apartment out of his pocket and handed them to her.

'So you're not planning on keeping me locked up inside all day, then?' she asked in as jovial a tone as she could muster.

'Of course not,' he said, waving away her words as if they were completely ridiculous.

Her skin prickled as she remembered how reluctant he'd been to introduce her to Hugo as his wife earlier, but she bit her tongue. She really didn't want to have a row with him on their wedding day. Not that it seemed they were actually going to celebrate it in any way.

This was confirmed when Xavier said, 'Well, I've a lot of work to do today so I'll let you get settled in. There's food in the fridge if you want to eat in tonight.'

Disappointment trickled through her. 'We won't be eating together?'

'Not tonight. I need to deal with something that's just cropped up at work right away.' He gestured towards his phone. 'I'll put your bags in your apartment and catch up with you tomorrow.'

'No, don't worry, I can take them.'

He paused, then nodded distractedly, and she watched him walk away and mount the stairs, heading up the wide staircase to the landing.

She suddenly felt very small and alone in the huge, dark house.

Looking down at the sheath dress she'd made especially for the ceremony out of one of her mother's old dresses, she felt a heavy sense of trepidation sink through her.

No, Soli, don't let it get to you.

Why she'd thought she needed to look good for this farce of a wedding today, she had no idea now. But it had been important to her to make an effort, even if Xavier hadn't appreciated it. He'd not said a word about how she looked.

She hadn't sewed her own clothes for a very long time, but being strapped for cash and not wanting to waste money on buying a proper wedding dress, even a second-hand one, she'd decided to make her own. She'd worked for three nights straight on it, and was really pleased with the results. Whilst working on it she'd remembered how much she'd enjoyed designing and making her own clothes before her mother had become too ill to look after herself and her father had died, requiring her to step into his role as carer, parent and breadwinner. Experiencing that had made her appreciate just how hard he'd worked to keep them all in the lifestyle she'd taken for granted. She wished fervently now that she'd had the opportunity to tell him how grateful she was to him for providing that for her.

She hoped he would have been proud of her for what she was doing here – making sure that her sister and mother were well looked after.

The way she needed to look at it was that Xavier was providing her with a unique opportunity to set them all up for the rest of their lives.

All she had to do was make sure she didn't do anything to jeopardise it.

5

FRUSTRATION (UK)/TROUBLE (US) – ROLL A SIX
BEFORE YOU CAN MAKE A MOVE.

The next morning Xavier came down to the kitchen at 7 a.m. to find to his relief that it was empty of his new wife. He'd been hoping that Soli wasn't an early riser, and wouldn't expect to have breakfast with him, so he could continue with his usual morning routine of sitting at the kitchen table and reading the news on his tablet whilst sipping his first cup of coffee of the day in peace.

It looked as if he was in luck.

As he set up the coffee machine, he noticed some cake tins and spatulas and a few bags of ingredients on the worktop. The sight of them sitting in what he thought of as his personal space sent a tingle of annoyance through him.

Telling himself to relax, he tamped down on his irritation, knowing he was going to have to get used to sharing his house with Soli for the next year and getting uptight about a few pieces of kitchen equipment lying around wasn't a good way to start. Anyway, it needed to look as if she lived in this house, he reminded himself, so having a few of her things scattered around would actually be a good thing.

He was just pouring the coffee into a mug when there was the sound of footsteps behind him and he spun around to see Soli standing in the doorway wearing a slouchy pair of pyjamas with a cartoon character on the front and her hair wild and sticking up around her head.

'Morning,' she said, hiding a yawn behind her hand. 'You're up bright and early.'

'I always leave at this time,' he said, averting his gaze as the idea of seeing her as she'd just rolled out of bed suddenly felt way too intimate.

'So, you don't have time to have breakfast with me?' she asked, moving towards the kettle, which she flicked on to boil.

'No, sorry. I need to leave in a minute.'

'Oh, okay.'

She looked disappointed, but he pushed aside the sting of guilt this brought about. He couldn't just change his routine to fit in with her. She'd need to work around him.

As if she'd sensed this, she leant back against the work surface, smiled at him and said, 'Perhaps we could spend some time together this evening instead? It'd be nice to get to know you a bit better since we'll be sleeping under the same roof for the next year. We could spend a bit of time drawing up a list of dos and don'ts for the relationship.'

He frowned as the uncomfortable reality of having someone at home waiting for him every night struck him. 'Yes, of course, but perhaps not tonight. I have a really heavy day at work, and I'll want to relax this evening. Once my workload's calmed down a bit we'll have plenty of time to do that.'

'Perhaps we could just play a board game or two, then. It'll be a fun, unpressurised way to learn more about each other,' she suggested. 'They're great icebreakers and it'll give us something else to concentrate on so we can chat freely. Our cafe is a popular destination for first dates precisely because of that. At least it used to be.' A frown flickered across her face. 'I'll cook us a light meal and we can play afterwards?' she suggested brightly.

His phone had beeped for the third time in as many minutes and he plucked it out of his pocket distractedly and glanced at the screen, seeing with a wave of concern that it was a message from his financial director. There must be an urgent issue for him to get in contact before the working day had begun. He glanced up from the screen to see Soli was looking at him with a questioning expression. 'Er, yes, okay. I should be back by about eight o'clock,' he said, wondering what could have happened for Rob to try him three times already.

'It'll be useful for us to know what makes each other tick,' she added.

'Yes. Quite right. We'll need to put up a good front at Hugo and Veronica's party and it'll help to be prepared for that,' he said with a sigh, running his hand over his jaw as the idea of it sent a twinge of tension up his back.

Would they really believe he'd married someone like Soli of his own free will? She really didn't dress, or act, like the type of woman he usually dated.

'I've been thinking about your question – about what you're going to do during the day when you're not working at the cafe.'

'Oh, yes?'

'I'm going to arrange for a monthly stipend to be put into your bank account which you can use to go shopping for new clothes and book hair and beauty appointments and the like. Those sorts of things ought to keep your free days busy enough and they'll be practically expected of a woman who's married to me and not working full-time, so it'll fit our story.'

She lifted a hand to smooth down her wild curls, then adjusted her pyjama top, her brow creasing into a bewildered sort of frown. 'Okay. Well, thanks.'

Feeling satisfied with this act of generosity, he cleared away his empty mug and gave her one last nod before striding out of the house and setting off for the office, feeling a strange sense of relief at having something to focus on outside of Soli and his brand-new marriage.

* * *

Soli finally let out the sigh of frustration she'd been holding in as the front door slammed shut behind Xavier.

Well, that had been an incredibly exasperating meet-up.

Awkward didn't even cover it.

It was clear he wanted them to look like a convincing couple at the party, but he seemed reluctant to actually spend any time with her.

Work, apparently, was going to take precedence.

Her heart sank at the anticipation of the fight she might have on her hands to get his full attention.

She shook off her worry. She'd find a way to make it work. Her family was relying on her and there was no way she was going to let them down now.

Pouring herself a reviving cup of coffee, she mulled over what he'd said to her just before he'd left. She really hadn't expected him to give her even more money – not that it wasn't welcome. She'd been acutely aware as she'd hung up her clothes in the wardrobe in her room that the sort of things she wore – mostly high street store outfits or things she'd picked up from a great little vintage clothes stall in Camden Market – probably wouldn't look quite right for someone married to Xavier McQueen, but his insinuation that she wasn't the sleek, sophisticated-looking woman he'd hoped for in a partner had still stung a little.

Not that she couldn't fix that if she splashed the cash around a bit.

It was going to feel pretty strange spending his money on frivolous things like that though, and she was going to have to get over that. If he was happy to give it to her, she should just be grateful for it.

She took a breath and straightened her spine, imagining herself into the role of the lady of the house.

The first thing she needed to do today was plan what she was going to make for their 'getting to know each other' meal. She wanted it to be something that looked as if she'd made a bit of effort, which of course actually meant making a lot of effort. Despite the fact they were only pretending, for the sake of her pride she wanted to be as good a partner as she could be.

Perhaps she could do steak with a peppercorn sauce and some lovely fresh seasonal vegetables. And Dauphinoise potatoes. Her sister loved it when she made that dish – which wasn't often because it was pretty labour intensive.

Yes, something like that perhaps. And she'd make a dessert from scratch too. Something with lots of fresh fruit, like a summer pudding.

Her spirits rose again.

While she was out shopping for all the ingredients she could pick up a couple of board games for them to play this evening too. Games that might lead them to interesting discussions and help them to get to know each other a bit better.

With a sense of positivity and purpose surging through her now, she sat down at the table and began to make a list, planning a wonderful evening of food and entertainment for her and her new husband.

It would be great to finally feel as if she was on top of things and acting like the kind of daughter her father always wanted to have.

Yup, she was a grown-up now and determined to prove to Xavier that he'd made a good choice in her and that it would be money well-spent.

He was going to be so pleased he'd married her.

* * *

It was ten-thirty before Xavier made it home that evening, after having to deal with the crisis at work that had kept him, his PA and his financial director in the office, scrambling to close a property deal that they'd been working on for the last three months.

It had been a taxing day, but Xavier was pleased with the way it had gone in the end. He felt buzzed with success as he let himself in through his front door and made his way across the entrance hall towards the back of the house.

Striding into his kitchen, he experienced a shiver of disquiet as something niggled at the back of his brain.

He'd not even had a chance to let Soli know he'd be back late; in fact, he'd been so engrossed in what he was doing he'd not noticed how late it was until his PA had jokily pointed out they should eat before all the takeaway outlets shut for the night, but he'd figured it wouldn't matter. Soli had plenty of things to entertain her here in the house and she seemed like the resourceful type.

After flicking on the kettle, he leant back against the kitchen counter and took a moment to look around the kitchen. There was something different in here, he was sure of it. It smelt different. A bit like the French restaurant he loved to go to on the bank of the Thames in Southwark. Garlicky and delicious.

The kettle boiled and he made himself a cup of tea, lifting the teabag out with the spoon after swishing it around in the boiling water for a few seconds. He never had the patience to let tea brew properly. When he lifted up the lid of the food-waste bin to dispose of the teabag, the garlicky smell grew even stronger and he paused, staring down inside the bin's depths. It looked as though there was a whole meal in there – what looked like Dauphinoise potatoes and cooked vegetables. What was Soli doing throwing so much food away? How wasteful.

And then it struck him and his stomach turned over with unease. She'd made dinner for him, and he'd not turned up for it. He hadn't even messaged to let her know he'd be too late to eat with her.

He snapped the bin lid shut and stepped away from it, feeling a strange mixture of self-righteousness and guilt. It wasn't as though he'd deliberately not turned up for the 'getting to know each other' dinner, he'd just forgotten about it. Work had had to take precedence today; it had been imperative to get on top of the problem before it had snowballed.

He'd explain all that to her tomorrow and apologise for missing dinner. There was no point in feeling guilty about it though. They had plenty of time to get to know each other and she'd have to get used to him having to work late without giving her any notice. That was how his life worked, and he wasn't about to change it for someone who was fundamentally in his employ.

She'd understand that.

Frankly, he was paying her a hefty chunk of money to understand and accept that.

With that assuring thought in mind he added a splash of milk to his tea then took it through to the sitting room to drink it, determined to enjoy a few minutes of his evening before he had to retire to bed.

* * *

When Soli turned up in the kitchen at seven o'clock the next morning, hoping to catch Xavier before he went to work, she was frustrated to find he'd already been and gone.

Had he done it on purpose, so he didn't have to see her?

She'd been disappointed and a bit hurt when he hadn't come home in time to eat the food she'd spent so much time and energy on, but she'd tried not to take it to heart. She'd decided to give him the benefit of the doubt and assume he'd just forgotten about it.

And her.

The uncomfortable twisting sensation that she'd experienced when she'd finally accepted he wasn't coming home last night reappeared.

She needed to get a grip. There were bound to be a few misunderstandings until they got to know each other better. He was a very busy man who ran his own company, so of course he was going to be working long hours and would be prone to forgetting she was at home, waiting for him.

But the dissenting voice in her head whispering that he was deliberately avoiding her wouldn't shut up.

She felt wired and restless now, as if there was something portentous in the air.

Perhaps it was the ghost of Xavier's great-aunt who had come to check up on the state of the marriage and was most displeased with what she saw.

Not that I blame you, Aunt Faith – I'd be pretty annoyed too if I found out he was playing the system to get round my wily attempt to force him to emotionally connect with life.

By eight o'clock that evening she'd just about given up hope of him appearing for dinner again and was about to start making enough food for one when she heard the front door open, then slam closed.

Heart thumping hard, she waited with bated breath to see whether he'd come to try and find her in the kitchen.

When he appeared in the doorway he seemed almost shocked to see her, as if he'd completely forgotten he had a wife.

'Soli, hi,' he said, frowning at her.

Steeling herself against a wave of disquiet, she said, 'Hi. How was your day?'

Oh, man, why did she feel so awkward talking to him? Perhaps because he was still frowning at her as if wondering what she was still doing here.

'It was fine,' he said distractedly, glancing around the kitchen.

'You're back late again.' She forced herself to smile graciously then waited to see whether this would trigger an apology for missing the dinner she'd made him the night before.

He ran a hand over his eyes and let out a sigh. 'Yes. It's not an uncommon occurrence.'

'I see.' So she wasn't getting an apology, then.

'How was your day?' he asked instead.

He still wasn't looking at her though; instead his gaze ran over the kitchen surfaces where she'd left some of her cake-making equipment.

'Pretty good, thanks,' she replied, pleased that he'd at least asked about her, even if he wasn't entirely engaged in the conversation.

'Are you planning on making stock for the cafe here?' he asked abruptly, the terseness in his tone shooting a shiver of discomfort down her spine.

'No, this is just some of my baking stuff from home. You don't mind if I keep it in here, do you?'

He seemed to seriously consider this request for a second or two as if deciding whether he'd be prepared to share the space with her. 'Sure. Why not?' he said eventually.

'Thanks,' she said, slightly discomfited, hoping he wasn't going to be this possessive about the rest of the house. Clearly, he wasn't used to having someone invading his territory.

Perhaps a goodwill gesture would make him more tolerant of her presence here.

'You know, I make a mean chocolate fudge cake. It's a particular favourite in the cafe. I can make one for you, if you like. It's yummy.'

She looked at him expectantly, hoping for some spark of interest.

'No. Thanks. I'm not a big fan of desserts.'

The pleasure she'd initially felt at the thought of spending time with him tonight was rapidly draining out of her.

'Oh. Okay.' She forced an undaunted smile, despite the sting of rejection she felt. 'No problem.' She swallowed. 'Have you eaten supper? I can make us some chilli. I've got all the ingredients right here.'

'No. Thanks,' he said again. 'I had a late lunch and I've got a few calls to make to the US, so it'll be a while before I'm done. You go ahead and eat without me.' He gave her a curt nod, then turned to leave the room.

The last dregs of her optimism drained away, leaving her totally deflated.

His business-like attitude towards her was seriously denting her excitement at living here with him. It was becoming starkly clear that he didn't want to spend any time with her and that he was deadly serious about keeping their relationship emotion-free.

Turning to stare down at the chopping board and the pile of ingredients for the food she didn't really feel like eating any more, she was just about to pick up the knife to start chopping enough onions for one portion, determined not to let him totally disturb her equilibrium, when she realised he was still in the room.

When she turned to look at him, she saw he was leaning against the door-jamb, watching her with a thoughtful expression on his face.

'I'm sorry I forgot about our "getting to know each other" dinner last night,' he said when he noticed her questioning eyebrow.

He didn't exactly sound sorry though. In fact, from the tone of his voice she got the impression he was actually quite irritated about having to explain himself.

'There's a good chance I won't be around at regular times in the evenings so don't worry about making food for me. I'll eat when I get in,' he went on when she didn't react right away.

So, she was going to be eating on her own every evening? How horrible. She hated the thought of sitting in this huge empty house all on her own, night after night, not having anyone to talk to. She was so used to being around people all day in the cafe and then chatting to her mum and sister over their family meals, it made her spirits sink to think she'd miss out on all that life while she was here.

For a whole year.

Her stomach knotted at the thought of it.

'You know, this house is such a big, lonely place for one person. Perhaps your great-aunt wanted you to get married and raise a family here so you're not on your own all the time,' she muttered, unable to keep her agitated thoughts to herself any longer.

She saw his shoulders stiffen and the air felt suddenly leaden with tension.

'Yes, well, she'll have to be forever disappointed in me for not having children, I'm afraid,' he said tersely.

'You don't want kids?' She was surprised to hear that.

'No.'

'Why not?'

'Because they're an inconvenience. They mess up your life.'

The bluntness of his tone bothered her.

'You really believe that?'

'Yes.'

But she could have sworn she saw a hint of uncertainty in his eyes. Just for a second.

'That's sad.'

'Sad? Why?' He was scowling at her now as if she was talking utter nonsense.

She shrugged. 'I don't know. I guess I can imagine you being a great dad.'

He looked at her steadily for a couple more beats and she got the feeling he was trying to decide how to handle this without it turning into a big deal.

'Well, thanks. But I don't think I'm the sort of person who could give a kid the kind of love they need.'

'Because your parents didn't give it to you?' she blurted without thinking, her frustration at his aloofness getting the better of her.

Exasperation flashed across his face, but he covered it quickly. 'I'd rather not talk about my parents.'

'Okay. Sorry.' But she didn't feel sorry, she felt annoyed with him for being so obstructive. Was he going to treat her like this for the entire year? Perhaps he'd hoped she'd squirrel away in her downstairs bedroom like an animal in a cage, never asking any awkward questions or getting in his way and only showing herself when he summoned her.

He must have seen the irritation on her face because he blinked in surprise. 'Anyway, I have a lot to do this evening,' he said, to her mounting ire. 'I'll leave you to it.'

Before she could utter another word, he strode out of the room, leaving her alone.

Again.

6

ARTICULATE – USE WORDS CLEVERLY TO FIGURE
OUT WHAT YOUR PARTNER IS TRYING TO TELL YOU.

The next few days followed a similar pattern, with Soli barely catching Xavier for two minutes over his morning coffee before he left for work and then him coming home at random times in the evening, regularly texting her to let her know he wouldn't be back in time for supper and to eat without him.

As her anxiety grew about how they would fare at the impending party, her focus frayed, making it increasingly difficult to concentrate on the marketing she had planned for the cafe.

So, when Friday night came around she crossed her fingers that Xavier would be back at a reasonable hour and finally willing to give her a bit of his precious time so she could finally put her mind at rest.

But when he walked in after nine o'clock he only poked his head into the sitting room, where she'd been trying to distract herself by half watching TV and half checking social media, and said a curt 'hello' before excusing himself to go up to his office.

Having sat on her own, fretting, as she drained a large glass of wine, Soli suddenly found she'd had enough of being ignored.

Springing up off the sofa, she ran into the hallway, where Xavier was already mounting the stairs, his long legs making short work of the winding staircase.

'Xavier!' she shouted, determined to get his attention before he disappeared on her again.

He stopped climbing and turned to look back down on her with a frown of surprise.

'Look,' she said, throwing up her hands in exasperation, 'I appreciate you're busy, but how am I supposed to convincingly pretend I'm your wife – someone that loves you and knows you intimately – if you won't even talk to me?' She held up both hands, palms forward. 'Can you please just give me half an hour of your time? Is that really too much to ask?'

He was looking at her now as if completely stunned by her outburst.

'I'm sorry to snap,' she said quickly, worried that she'd gone too far in her agitation, 'but I've reached my limit of pretending not to mind you treating me like a piece of furniture.' She tried to smile but her mouth refused to play ball. Instead, to her horror, her muscles began to tug downwards at each side and her throat constricted painfully as she fought back tears.

But she wasn't going to cry. No way. She was going to be an adult about this.

'If you really want us to appear like a proper couple you're going to have to let me in a bit,' she pointed out in a measured tone.

A muscle in his jaw flickered, but after a few seconds of seeming to seriously contemplate what she was saying he gave her a curt nod of agreement.

'Okay, then. And how do you propose I do that?'

She moved to the bottom of the stairs and leant on the newel post, looking up at him, a mixture of excitement and relief surging through her. 'There's this game I've played at a party which helps you get to know the other guests better. First of all, you have to look into each other's eyes for three minutes – to begin to feel more comfortable with that person in a physical sense.' She paused, gauging his reaction.

'Go on,' was all he said, walking down one step towards her.

'Then we ask each other a set of questions which are meant to give us some insight into each other's lives – how we see the world, what makes us feel good and bad. Personal self-disclosure, I think it's called.'

'Right.' He seemed less certain about this, but he hadn't said no, so she decided to forge on.

'The shared vulnerability is supposed to make us feel closer and help us trust each other more. I appreciate this is a bit of an ask at this early stage, but I think it'll be a great way to get comfortable with each other pretty quickly, especially since we don't have a lot of time to do that, what with you being so busy at work.'

She tried to keep her scepticism out of her voice about how busy she thought he really was, as opposed to how he'd probably been using it as an excuse to avoid her, but from the twitch in his eyebrow she could tell she'd failed.

'Okay, Soli, fine.' He rubbed his hand over his jaw. 'I guess we should do this now since Hugo and Veronica's party is tomorrow.' He walked down the rest of the stairs to where she stood. 'Where do you want to do it?'

'The sitting room would be good. Somewhere we can sit comfortably.'

'Okay. Lead the way,' he said.

She ignored the weariness in his voice, determined not to give him an excuse not to go through with this. Hopefully once they started communicating properly, he'd start to relax around her.

In the sitting room she chose the three-seater sofa and sat down on it, patting the cushion next to her to encourage him to sit close by.

He followed her suggestion and turned to face her, laying his arm along the top of the sofa and looking anything but excited about the prospect of doing this.

'Okay, I'm going to set the timer going, then we have to sit looking at each other's faces, particularly the eyes, until the beeper goes.' She shifted in her seat, trying to ignore the wave of heat rising up her neck at the thought of actually doing this now with Xavier.

'Are you ready?' she asked him.

'As I'll ever be,' he drawled.

'Okay, then, I'm starting the timer – now,' she said, tapping on the screen of her phone.

Turning to face him and settling her body into a comfortable position, she fought back a ridiculous urge to giggle, knowing it would spoil the exercise before they'd even started, and took a breath, locking her eyes with his.

He nodded as if resigned to letting this happen and looked back at her with that shrewd, intelligent gaze of his.

Soli swallowed, suddenly acutely aware of every breath she took, every facial muscle she moved. It was intensely intimate, having him looking at her so thoroughly without a break, but she was determined not to look away.

All the hairs on her body stood up and a hot tingle rushed over her skin as the seconds ticked by slowly, but she still didn't look away.

He really was an immensely attractive man, she mused as she gazed at his olive skin with its five o'clock shadow and his long, dark lashes that almost brushed his cheeks every time he blinked.

She became aware of some strange feeling building inside her, something that made her pulse jump in her throat, but before she had a chance to figure out exactly what it meant the timer went off, making them both jump.

'Sorry, I didn't realise I'd set the volume that high,' she said, flustered and grabbing for the phone with fumbling fingers. Finally managing to turn it off, she turned back to him and shot him an apologetic grin.

'Well, that was fun,' she joked.

His mouth actually twitched up at the corner at that, which she considered a personal victory. Of sorts.

'At least we'll be able to describe each other's faces to an outsider in detail now too,' she said, acutely aware of a telltale wobble in her voice. 'You know, I hadn't realised your eyes had yellow flecks in them; I thought it was just a lighter shade of green. Oh, and how did you get the small scar by your lip? It's so tiny I hadn't noticed it till now.'

'I fell off my bike here in the garden when I was eight,' he said, lifting his hand to touch the scar she'd mentioned, almost absently. 'Aunt Faith bought it for my birthday, and the front brakes were really fierce. I went right over the handlebars.'

'Ouch!' she said, with a grin.

'Precisely,' he agreed, his mouth twitching upwards again.

Yes, progress! It seemed the forced intimacy had opened something up a crack between them. She just needed to press her advantage now and get him talking to her some more.

'Okay, then, now we've done that let's move on to the questions. I'll ask you some first, okay?'

He began to frown, but seemed to change his mind. 'Sure. Fire away.' Shuffling back against the sofa cushions, he crossed his arms in front of him and gave her his full attention.

Soli felt herself flush again under his gaze, but tried not to let it distract her.

'What would be a perfect day for you?' she asked as a starter question.

'Hmm.' He rubbed his hand over his jaw again, but in a thoughtful manner this time.

'Well, I rarely get the chance for a lie-in, so I'd have one of those.'

Soli tried hard not to picture him lying naked and rumpled in bed. And failed.

'Then I'd have a long, lazy breakfast and perhaps a walk across the heath. Maybe have a swim in the lake and a picnic lunch.'

From the faraway look in his eyes now, she got the impression he was actually enjoying thinking this up. The thought of it warmed her.

'In the afternoon I'd go and play tennis then head out for a slap-up meal in town.'

'Wow, that all sounds great,' she said with a grin. 'And when was the last time you spent a day doing things like that?'

This seemed to stump him. 'I don't think I've ever had a day like that. I've always been too busy with work or had other social engagements.'

'Oh. What a shame.'

'Yes, I guess it is,' he said, shrugging his shoulder.

There was a small pause where neither of them said anything.

'When was the last time you sang in front of someone?' Soli asked, to fill the silence.

'Never,' he said with a shake of his head.

'Really? Never?'

'I'm not really into performing,' he said with finality to his tone.

'Oh. Okay, then,' she said, recognising his need to move on.

'How about this: if you could choose one ability that you don't already have, what would it be?'

'To predict the future,' he said with confidence.

Soli thought this was interesting. It clearly pointed to a need for complete control.

'What are you most grateful for?'

He paused infinitesimally before replying, 'My health, wealth and happiness.'

Glib, but okay.

'What would you never joke about?'

'Money.' There was no pause before that answer.

'Is there something you've always dreamt of doing but have never got round to? Tell me about it, then tell me why you haven't done it yet.'

'Hmm.' This gave him pause. 'I think I'm doing what I dreamt of. I wanted to run my own company and live in this house.'

'Okay. Well... well done,' she said with a smile. 'What's your biggest accomplishment?'

'Same answer. My company and finding a way to live in this house.' He looked particularly pleased with himself for that answer.

'Tell me about a happy memory from your school days.'

Suddenly the buoyant atmosphere seemed to drop like a stone.

'I can't think of one right now,' he said tersely, his gaze skimming away from hers now.

There was something heartbreakingly raw about the way he said this, but she didn't press it. From the way his shoulders had stiffened she got the impression he'd happily call an end to the session if she did and that was the last thing she wanted when he was finally starting to open up to her a little.

'What has been your most embarrassing moment?' she asked with a smile, hoping to flip the mood, but was a little taken aback to see the expression in his eyes harden at this. 'It can be something really silly,' she added quickly, desperately trying to rescue the lightness they'd had previously.

'Pass. I can't think of anything right now,' he said again, his tone warning her not to push it. Clearly, she was treading on dodgy ground.

Okay. She could come back to that another time. She didn't want to ruin the progress they'd made. But something still pushed her to ask the next question anyway.

'What's your relationship with your mother like now you're grown up?'

The light went out of his eyes. She realised with a shiver of disappointment that she'd blown it and that he'd probably clam up completely now, but to her surprise he didn't. Instead, he hooked an arm across the back of the sofa again and looked directly into her eyes as if actively deciding not to dodge her interest in the question any more. Perhaps he was hoping she'd leave him alone if he finally gave her an answer to it.

'I don't really know her, to be honest. We have very little contact these days. She's not exactly the maternal type. I think she fell pregnant with me by accident – at least, that's what I overheard one day when my great-aunt and a friend of hers were chatting. Apparently, my father convinced her to keep me, but she and I never really bonded. Not that my relationship with my father was much better. He was always being sent away overseas with work. He was a foreign diplomat. My mother often went with him, but they kept me here in England at boarding school. It was for my own good, apparently, so I wouldn't feel unsettled.'

From the expression on his face she gleaned that it had actually had the opposite effect. No wonder he was so attached to this house. It seemed to be the only place he'd ever felt secure. She couldn't imagine how horrible it must have been not to be allowed to live with your family. There were so many good memories from her own childhood, she'd be devastated not to have had the opportunity to experience them. Some of them were only snatched, random moments in her memory, but they still held so much meaning for her. They'd helped her grow and form as a person, and the knowledge that she'd be able to come home to her family and a safe, loving environment every day after school had kept her going through her most taxing years.

'I suspect it was really because they thought I'd cramp their style if I was living with them,' Xavier went on, his eyes taking on a faraway, troubled look now. 'They were always big socialisers, according to my great-aunt...' He paused, as if weighing up whether he wanted to say the next thing out loud, obviously deciding that he did when he added, 'And not exactly faithful to each other.'

'Oh. I'm sorry to hear that. It must have been really unsettling for you,' she said quietly.

He looked at her again, his expression softer now with what she thought might be appreciation for her understanding.

'It wasn't great, but then no one's life is perfect, right?'

'True,' she said, giving him a supportive smile.

There was another heavy pause as they just looked at each other again and Soli felt a strange sort of pulse beat between them.

'Any more?' Xavier said, breaking the tension.

'Any more what?' she asked, a little shaken by the atmosphere that had formed.

'Questions,' he said pointedly.

'Oh! Yes. Okay.' Pulling herself together, she asked, 'What would you regret not having said to someone if you were to unexpectedly die this evening?'

He raised a wry eyebrow, his eyes twinkling with mirth.

'Don't worry, I'm not thinking about doing you in,' she added with a grin, then muttered, 'yet,' waggling her eyebrows in jest.

He came really close to properly smiling at that and her heart did a little dance of joy.

'Hmm, I don't know,' he said thoughtfully. 'I guess I wish I'd had a chance to tell my great-aunt how much I appreciated her taking me under her wing like she did. I don't know what would have happened to me if she hadn't.'

Soli became aware of tears pooling in her eyes. 'I'm glad you had her. She sounds like an amazing woman.'

'She was.'

Blinking away her tears and pointing at her eyes, then wafting her hands at either side of them with a strained smile of embarrassment, she asked, 'When did you last cry in front of someone?'

He frowned, but didn't meet her eyes. 'I'm not a crier.'

'Really? You never cry?'

'Not in front of other people, no.' He shifted a little in his seat and crossed his arms. 'And it's been years since I cried on my own.'

'Oh. Okay, then.' There was something so heart-wrenching about this, it actually caused her physical pain deep in her chest. How awful that he didn't feel he could express his sorrow in front of someone else.

'I cry in front of people all the time,' she said with a self-deprecating grin. 'I find it cathartic. I always feel better afterwards, though sometimes I'm embarrassed by how easily I do it. I cry at anything even remotely sad,' she said, feeling tears pushing at the backs of her eyes again just from thinking about it.

His shoulders had stiffened as if he was really uncomfortable now and he glanced down at his watch, as if wanting to escape from the conversation.

This was confirmed when he said, 'Anyway, Soli, it's been an interesting exercise, but I really do have some work to do this evening, so I'm going to say goodnight.'

'Okay,' she said, watching him get up from the sofa, feeling a swell of satisfaction from getting as far as she had.

It was early days yet, but at least she knew a bit more about him now.

His emotional unavailability made more sense now she knew more about how he'd been ignored by his parents during his childhood. She felt truly sorry for the poor, lonely little boy he must have been growing up, not having a family who loved him or a home to come back to during his breaks from school. What must that do to a child? To not feel wanted by the people who were supposed to love you unconditionally?

It was a horrible thought.

Well, she'd make sure she did her very best to support him in the months to come. She'd need to be careful not to get dragged into an emotional quicksand where Xavier was concerned – it wouldn't be sensible to allow herself to actually fall for the guy, she reminded herself with a strange pulse of panic – but she could be a friend to him, as he'd suggested.

Yes, that was exactly what they both really needed at this juncture in their lives.

A good friend.

7

WOULD I LIE TO YOU? – KEEP YOUR COOL AND THINK QUICKLY TO WIN THIS GAME.

Xavier slept badly that night and woke up later than his usual 6 a.m. start.

After having that conversation with Soli, his dreams had been tangled with memories of his time at boarding school – feeling isolated and humiliated when he'd been the only boy whose parents hadn't turned up to watch an end-of-term performance before they all left for the Christmas break. It had then changed to him standing in the mostly empty register office with Soli. In the dream they were reciting the lines they'd been asked to say, except it wasn't the registrar conducting the service, it was Great-Aunt Faith, who was barking instructions at them as if they were disobedient children.

As he'd turned to apologise to Soli, he'd realised it wasn't her standing next to him after all – it was Harriet.

'Really, Xavier? You had to pay her to marry you? How pathetic,' she'd sneered at him and the ugly look of utter disdain on her face had woken him with a sickening jolt.

It had been so vivid and had drawn such a strong emotional response from him he felt exhausted now, as if he'd not slept a wink all night.

Remembering with relief that it was the weekend, he allowed himself to lie in bed and read the news on an app on his phone, determinedly pushing the unsettling echoes of the dream out of his mind, before finally dragging himself out of bed for a shower then heading down to the kitchen for breakfast.

He'd just got the coffee machine set up and running when the buzzer for the entry phone at the front gate went.

Frowning to himself and wondering who the hell would be so uncouth as to turn up uninvited at this hour on a Saturday morning, he picked up the handset and snapped, 'Yes?'

'Mr McQueen? This is Samuel Pinker. I've been employed by your great-aunt's estate to visit you and your wife at home in accordance with her will.'

Heat rushed across his skin, quickly followed by a wave of cold panic that made his hair stand on end. So they were being checked up on already?

'Okay. Well, you'd better come in,' he said, forcing his tone to sound jovial and upbeat. 'Solitaire is still in bed, I'm afraid. It's a little early for her, so you'll need to give me a few moments to rouse her.'

'No problem,' the voice of Pinker said over the phone. 'I have a quick call to make so I'll park in your driveway and give you a knock in five minutes, if that suits you?'

'That would be fine,' Xavier said steadily.

'Thank you,' the man replied.

Xavier pressed the button to release the gate, then dashed out of the kitchen and down the corridor to Soli's room, where he banged hard on the door.

It was a full minute before he was able to rouse her.

'Xavier? What's the matter?' she asked, hiding a yawn behind her hand and looking a little bewildered to see him standing there.

'There's someone here from my great-aunt's solicitor's office to check up on us. You need to get dressed. Quickly,' he said, determinedly trying not to notice how appealing she looked, all bed-rumpled and sleepy.

Her eyes sprang open at that, and she did a little nervous jiggle on the spot. 'Should I get dressed?' she asked, her voice wobbling with panic.

'No,' he said, thinking it would seem more realistic if it looked as though she'd just got out of bed. 'But perhaps put a robe over your pyjamas?'

'I don't have one!' she said, flustered.

'There's one on the back of my bedroom door. Go and put that on. It'll look better if you come from upstairs anyway. As soon as you hear me open the door, come down. Okay?'

She looked slightly terrified now. 'What am I meant to say to him? We haven't worked it out yet!'

'Don't worry. Let me do the talking. Just try and make it look as though you like me and find me attractive,' he said, flipping her a wry smile.

She nodded jerkily. 'Okay. I can do that.'

There was a strange, zingy tension suddenly between them, but he brushed it off, not having the time to consider what it might mean.

Two minutes after she'd dashed upstairs, the doorbell went, and Xavier took a deep, steadying breath before going to answer it.

Their visitor was a portly man, with a shock of russet hair and a cheerful smile.

'Samuel Pinker,' he said, holding out a hand, which Xavier shook firmly.

'Good to meet you. Please come in.'

He guided the man into the hallway, just as Soli made a timely appearance at the top of the stairs.

The two men looked up at her as she descended, and Pinker once again held out his hand in greeting as Soli reached the bottom stair.

Soli, to her credit, appeared to be totally relaxed as she shook his hand and introduced herself, giving Pinker a warm smile that lit up her whole face.

Xavier's stomach did an odd swoop as he once again thought how attractive she looked with her wild curls framing her pretty face and her cheeks pink and a little sleep-creased. The robe she'd found in his bedroom was far too big for her, but it only enhanced how feminine and delicate she was.

He had the strangest compulsion to wrap his arms around her, to protect her from Pinker's searching gaze, but he held back, not wanting to spook her and give the two of them away.

To his surprise, Soli appeared to have the same urge to touch him, and he gave a small involuntary grunt of surprise as she walked straight up to him and slid her arms around his middle, pulling herself close so they were chest to chest. He looked down to see she was gazing adoringly into his eyes.

His heart did a three-hundred-and-sixty-degree turn.

Remembering the exercise they'd done only the night before, he maintained eye contact with her, immediately recalling that same close connection he'd experienced, so didn't even blink when she stood on tiptoe to plant a light, soft kiss on his mouth.

The sweet, sleep-warmed scent of her invaded his consciousness, making his senses reel and his body instinctively tighten with lust.

Ah, hell. If she pressed herself any closer to him there was a good chance this could turn into a very embarrassing moment indeed.

Luckily, she pulled away before he completely lost control of the situation and turned to smile at Pinker, who was watching them with a focused sort of smile on his face.

'Can I get you a cup of coffee, Mr Pinker?' she asked him. 'We were just about to have one.'

To Xavier's surprise, Pinker shook his head. 'No, thank you, Mrs McQueen. I only popped in so I could tick the "living together" box on the paperwork. It's very clear you both live here, what with me turning up at such an ungodly hour at the weekend and finding you in residence. I do apologise for any inconvenience caused – it's my job, you know?'

'Of course! We totally understand,' Soli said, with warmth in her voice.

'Well, I'll let you good people enjoy the rest of your morning,' Pinker said, tipping Soli a courteous nod and offering Xavier a smile. 'No doubt I'll see the two of you again at some point. Until then...' He made for the door, giving Xavier a nod of thanks when he opened it for him, and vanished outside.

Xavier waited until he saw Pinker's car pull out of the driveway before shutting the door with a sigh of relief and turning to face Soli.

'Well done,' he said, walking towards where she still stood by the stairs. 'I think we convinced him.'

Soli smiled back, looking a bit sheepish now. 'Sorry for kissing you like that without warning, but I thought it would look more authentic. It's the sort of thing I'd do if we were really married.'

'No problem,' he said, lifting a hand to touch his lips where the ghost of Soli's kiss still lingered. 'It's a good job you insisted on that eye-gazing thing yesterday – it made it a lot easier for me to look at you.'

'Thanks. I think,' Soli said, flashing him a rueful grin.

'I didn't mean...' He shook his head, irritated with himself. 'I meant it made it easier to be immediately intimate with each other.'

'I knew what you meant,' Soli said, widening her grin, evidently enjoying winding him up.

He couldn't help but smile back at her, a surge of relief-filled happiness appearing out of nowhere. Clearly, he'd made the right choice in Soli for his pretend wife. Her quick reaction today gave him confidence they'd actually be able to pull this thing off at the party this evening.

'Oh, wow!' Soli said loudly.

'What?' he asked, startled.

'Your smile. It's incredible. You should do that more often.'

'Uh, thanks.' He smiled again in a show of nonchalant acceptance, but her words had made a tingle shoot straight up his spine. No one had complimented him on his smile in a very long time. Perhaps because he hadn't had much to smile about.

They stood there, just looking at each other for a couple of beats, and once again Xavier had the weirdest feeling that Soli was someone he could really trust and rely on. Strangely – considering she was still practically a stranger to him – she was one of the few people he'd ever felt that about.

She looked back at him with curiosity in her eyes. And something else. Something that made his skin heat and his body tense with arousal.

He suddenly wanted to kiss her again, just to experience that same thrilling feeling of being connected.

No. No. Not a good idea.

Obviously, it had been much too long since he'd been physically involved with a woman if he was contemplating messing with this precariously balanced business relationship he'd negotiated so carefully.

'You know, it occurs to me that I didn't ask anything about you when we did that getting to know each other exercise last night,' he said, taking a deliberate step back away from her. 'Want to chat now over coffee?'

The look of surprise on her face made him feel equal parts amused and guilty and a hot sort of discomfort trickled through him. Apparently, she'd not expected him to take any interest in her as a person.

'Just in case we're caught out like that again,' he added quickly, not wanting her to read too much into his offer of friendship.

'Er... yes, sure. If you like,' she said, folding her arms around her middle and looking suddenly a little uncomfortable about standing in front of him in her nightwear.

'Feel free to get dressed first,' he said with a reassuring smile, 'but only if you want to. Don't do it for me.'

'Nah, I'm fine,' she said, letting her arms swing down to her sides and pushing back her shoulders. 'Let's do it now.'

He really liked her self-confidence.

So they started off by chatting about simple things like their favourite books and films and music, then they moved on to which countries they'd like to visit and why.

'So, it sounds like you haven't travelled much yet,' he said as she reeled off the long list of places to visit on her bucket list.

'I've not had much chance,' she said with a sad smile. 'Ever since my dad died, I've had to spend all my time working and looking after my mum and sister.'

'Yes, of course,' Xavier said, chastened. He'd almost forgotten how much she'd had to deal with during her relatively short life. 'That must have been pretty tough.'

'Yeah, it was at the beginning,' she said, hunching her shoulders, but maintaining her sunny smile. 'My mum got very depressed after we lost him and started really struggling with her Parkinson's, and Domino was too young to help out. She still needed someone to look after her and I was the only one available. It didn't leave a lot of time for me.'

'No. I bet,' was all he could muster in response. It made him realise how easy he'd had it being an only child with family money behind him. Glancing at his watch, he gave a start of surprise. He'd been enjoying chatting with her so much he'd not noticed how the time had flown. 'Hey, it's nearly lunchtime already.'

'Oh!' she said, looking slightly panicked. 'I'd better get dressed and grab some lunch. I have a hair appointment at two o'clock.'

Once she'd dashed off and changed her clothes they reconvened in the kitchen and ate their fill of the delicious food that Soli had loaded the fridge with – which mostly consisted of Mediterranean-inspired fare like brightly coloured salads, a cold meat platter and a range of healthy grains – before she excused herself to go to her appointment, leaving him on his own.

Experiencing a strange surge of energy once she'd gone, he took himself off for a long, hard session in the gym, followed by a lengthy swim in the pool.

Finally feeling as if he'd got past the odd edgy tension that had kept him moving, he went for a scorching hot shower, coming down from his bedroom to find a wonderful smell wafting from the direction of the kitchen.

Striding in, he found the room empty, though it was clear Soli had been in here recently because there were mixing bowls in the sink and a dusting of flour on the work surfaces. The smell seemed to be coming from the range oven and he peered through the glass to see a large cake rising inside its tin.

Despite having stuffed himself at lunchtime, he heard his stomach give a growl of hunger. He'd told her he didn't have much of a sweet tooth, but he'd make an exception for something that smelt that good.

'I thought we could take it to the party as a gift for your friends,' came a soft voice behind him and he spun around to see Soli standing in the doorway with a tentative smile on her face.

There was a strange rising sensation in his chest when he noticed how her wild curls had been tamed into sleek blonde waves, making her look a good few years older than she was. Not that he didn't like her usual hairstyle. In fact, he probably preferred her hair au naturel, but he appreciated the effort she'd gone to for the party.

'Your hair looks nice,' he croaked through a suddenly dry throat.

It must be the heat from the oven getting to him.

She gave him a wide, delighted smile. 'Thanks, I'm glad you like it.'

'Are you going to be wearing that later?' he asked jokily to distract himself from the inappropriate way his body seemed to be responding to her now, pointing to the bathrobe he'd loaned her that morning, which she had wrapped tightly around her.

She smiled back. 'I wasn't planning on it, no. I bought a dress especially for the occasion. I hope it's the right sort of thing.' He noticed her jaw twitch and realised she was probably as nervous about going tonight as he was.

'Don't worry, they're a friendly crowd, on the whole.' He took a stabilising breath. 'I probably ought to warn you that there's a good chance my ex, Harriet, might be there, and there could be a bit of tension.' He frowned, wondering how best to explain this without having to go into too much embarrassing detail. 'We didn't part on great terms.'

'Oh. I'm sorry to hear that. So it wasn't a mutual split, then?'

He looked at her steadily for a second, weighing up whether or not to answer that, before shaking his head. 'No. It was her choice. But I'm over it now.'

Soli's eyes narrowed as if suspicious of this bold statement. 'How long were you with her?'

'Four years. We met in our last year of university.'

The usual wave of hurt flooded through him at the thought of Harriet and all that had happened between them, but he was determined not to let seeing her again ruin his night tonight. He needed to concentrate on getting through this thing successfully with Soli and convincing his friends they were a real married couple in order to avoid any more personal humiliation. That had to be his top priority.

'Is there anything specific I need to know? So I don't make a faux pas if we meet her?' Soli asked, her expression open and her voice so kind it reached right inside him and tugged at his heart.

He almost told her everything, right there and then, but decided against it at the last second. She didn't need to know all the sordid details. It wasn't as if everyone would still be gossiping about it now. Surely they'd all moved on.

'No. I think it's probably best if we just avoid her. I don't want to cause a scene, especially not in front of Hugo and Veronica, who are friends with both of us,' he said stiffly.

'Okay. Well, thanks for the heads up.' She was looking at him now with a concerned expression, as if she suspected there was more to it than he was telling her.

Nothing, it seemed, got past Soli.

There was an awkward beat of silence where they both smiled at each other, and he couldn't help but think how pretty she looked. Her pupils seemed to dilate as she continued to maintain eye contact with him and she drew in a soft, breathy gasp, opening her lips a fraction as if she couldn't quite get enough air.

His gaze immediately moved to her mouth and he had to force himself not to start wondering what it would feel like to kiss those soft, inviting lips again.

'I should get the cake out of the oven before it burns,' she said a little over-brightly, jarring him out of his lascivious trance.

'Yes. Okay. You do that,' he said, a little rattled by his body's instinctive response to her. 'I'd better go and get ready for the party. We need to leave in about an hour.'

At the door he turned back to watch her as she busied herself around the kitchen, drawing in a great lungful of the delicious smell of the cake as she opened the oven door and bent down to lift it out.

'There's a good chance that won't make it out of the house,' he joked. 'It's altogether too tempting.'

She turned to give him a startled look, quickly recovering her composure when she realised he was talking about the cake. 'I thought you didn't like sweet things?'

He raised an eyebrow, tamping down on his amusement about the misinterpreted innuendo. It wasn't really appropriate to flirt with her when they were on their own. 'For that,' he nodded to the tin she had in her oven-gloved hands, 'I'll make an exception. It smells incredible.'

Her answering blush brought a smile to his lips, and he allowed himself to flip her one last grin before walking away to prepare for the party, hyper-aware of his blood pumping hard in his ears.

8

CLUEDO (UK)/CLUE (US) – UNCOVER THE CULPRIT WITH DEDUCTION AND GUILE.

It was more of a garden party than a posh evening do, as it turned out, which suited Soli just fine. It meant she was less likely to melt into a sweaty, nervous puddle as they mingled with the large throng of elegant, sophisticated guests.

To Soli, Xavier seemed completely at ease as they moved from group to group, received with a mix of exaggerated bonhomie and friendly curiosity. He gave a nod here and there, occasionally paused to introduce her, then politely excused them and moved swiftly on.

The comforting weight and heat of Xavier's arm around her waist kept her grounded as they circulated around the party and after a while she started to relax and chat with the people who asked kind, but slightly bemused questions of her, particularly about how she'd met Xavier. Once she'd given her answer about meeting him through the business, she quickly moved the focus of the conversation onto the other person, making sure to ask them lots of questions about themselves.

They'd been there for about twenty minutes without catching sight of the host or hostess, who according to one guest were either down in the wine cellar stocking up on booze or settling a tantrum-throwing child, when there was a shout from behind them. 'Xavier McQueen, where have you been hiding?'

They both turned away from the couple they were chatting with to see a tall, slim woman wearing a flowing cornflower-blue silk cocktail dress striding purposefully towards them. She pushed her long, sleek black hair away from her face as she got nearer and gave them a huge grin, her dark eyes sparkling with delight.

'Veronica. Lovely to see you,' Xavier said, taking a step towards her. Soli could tell from the smile in his voice that he was genuinely pleased to see her. But if that was the case, why had he not seen his friends for so long? He couldn't have been that busy with work, surely.

'I'm so pleased you came! I had a bet on with Hugo that you would. He owes me a fiver, oh, he of little faith!' She raised a playful eyebrow at Soli. 'My darling husband thought the two of you might be a bit too busy "being newlyweds".' She turned to give Xavier a playful wink. 'But I knew you wouldn't be so mean as to deny us your wonderful presence at such an important do. Five years we've been married, can you believe it?'

Without waiting for a response from him she turned to look at Soli with wide, discerning eyes. 'Now, who is this delightful creature? Introduce me to your cute-as-a-button new wife, Xavier.' She held out a manicured hand, which Soli shook, a little surprised by the strength of the woman's grip.

'This is Solitaire – Soli for short,' Xavier said. The sound of her name on his lips gave Soli a strange little shiver of delight. He had such a wonderful deep, gravelly voice – it always did something to her whenever he spoke.

'It's so wonderful to meet you,' Veronica said, pulling her in for an enveloping hug. 'What a gorgeous name!'

Soli believed she really meant it too – she didn't seem at all patronising or false; her smile and touch were too warm for that.

'Lovely to meet you too. Thanks so much for inviting us,' Soli said, returning Veronica's smile. 'What a beautiful garden you have,' she said, gesturing towards what must have been half an acre of land, with its vibrant borders of summer flowers in full bloom and its springy grass that her heels kept sinking into, rooting her to the spot.

'Oh! Thank you! We love being out here in the summer and it's great for the children when they need to burn off some steam. Which is all the time!' She laughed, then glanced at Xavier, her smile faltering as an expression that Soli couldn't quite read flashed across her face. But only for a second. Had she felt as if she'd put her foot in it with him for some reason?

'I probably should mention that we've invited Harriet and her partner here today,' Veronica said, her expression a bit strained now.

'I expected you would,' Xavier said in a neutral tone, though Soli could have sworn she felt him stiffen beside her.

'I just thought I'd warn you so it wouldn't be a shock if you saw her here. I understand you haven't been in touch since...' She broke off, glancing quickly at Soli before returning her gaze to him. 'I just mean I can understand why you kept a low profile after what happened,' Veronica finished in a sympathetic tone.

Soli stood motionless, listening intently, wondering what the heck she was missing here.

Xavier shrugged. 'I thought it'd be better to let Harriet feel as if she could still see her friends without me being around all the time,' he said gruffly. 'You were her friends first, after all.'

Was she imagining it, or was there a hint of pain in his voice? The very idea made her shiver with horror, and she experienced the strongest urge to wrap her arms around him, to let him know she was there for him and on his side should he need her. He froze for a second as she gave in to her instinct and slid her arm around his waist, but quickly relaxed again, pulling her closer in to his side.

Veronica smiled at the two of them, seeming to decide that Xavier must be over it. 'Well, I'm delighted that you have this gorgeous creature by your side now.' She gave Soli a warm smile, before moving her gaze back to Xavier.

'You know, there's a real spark between the two of you – something I never saw between you and Harriet. I always thought she was a bit too straight for you. In retrospect I'm sure getting married wasn't the right thing for either of you at the time. It was probably for the best that she called it off.'

Soli's heart gave an extra-hard thump in her chest. So, he'd nearly married Harriet, but she'd called it off?

There was an uncomfortable pause before Xavier cleared his throat and said, 'Yes, perhaps so. It would have been nice to have had more than an hour's notice that she'd changed her mind though.'

Soli's breath caught in her throat. So Harriet had dumped him at the altar! How humiliating for him. She couldn't imagine anything worse for someone as proud as Xavier. No wonder he'd been so determined not to get married again – and that his great-aunt had felt she'd had to go to such extremes to make him even consider it.

Not that he'd married her for love.

The thought made her stomach do a sickening sort of lurch.

'Oh, darling, I know.' It was Veronica's turn to sound uncomfortable now. 'It was a terrible thing to do to you, but I think she just panicked. She'd been feeling wobbly about it for a while, but Hugo and I persuaded her it was just pre-wedding jitters. I'm so sorry we didn't talk to you about it beforehand. Still, it's done now and you're happy with your lovely new wife,' Veronica said brightly, as if sensing the need to move the conversation onto safer ground. 'By the way, where did you two meet? I forgot to ask.'

'Through the business,' Xavier said in a confident tone that even had Soli convinced for a second.

Veronica smiled indulgently. 'You know, Xavier, I don't think I've ever seen you looking so relaxed. The two of you are obviously good for each other.'

Soli stood stock-still, her heart beating rapidly in her throat, wondering what on earth Xavier would say to that. She hoped with all her heart it would be something nice. It felt incredibly important at that moment that it was.

'Soli is really good for me,' he said, to her surprise. 'The first thing I noticed about her was how vibrant and upbeat she is. I find her positivity really inspiring, to be honest, because, as we know, I'm not always the sunniest of people.' The look of genuine approval on his face when he turned to look at her made Soli's tummy flutter with exhilaration.

Veronica gave a tinkling laugh. 'Don't do yourself down. You're a wonderful person and a great friend – when you deign to accept invitations from us.' She laughed again, but it was plain from her tone that she was genuinely joking around with him.

At that moment, a small child ran up to them, shouting, 'Mummy, Mummy!' and did a spectacular trip-dive just before reaching them, splashing her beaker full of blackcurrant juice all over Veronica's shoes.

There were a few seconds of noisy disruption as the child began to wail and Veronica half admonished, half comforted her.

Turning to them with a tearful child pressed up against her, she said, 'I'm so sorry, will you excuse me for a second? I'd better take her inside and get myself cleaned up. Don't run off, now, will you? I want to chat more later. It's been so long! I want to hear all about what you've been up to in the last few years, including all the details about your wedding.'

As soon as she was out of earshot Soli turned to look at Xavier, who was standing stiffly by her side, watching Veronica walk away with a frown on his face. 'So, it wasn't just your parents that let you down, it was your fiancée too,' she said quietly.

She waited, looking up at him expectantly, willing him to trust her and tell her the whole story.

His frown deepened, then he gave a curt nod.

So that was all she was getting? Her pulse rate soared as frustration shot through her.

'Why didn't you tell me Harriet stood you up at the altar?' she blurted into the silence, unable to hold on to her patience any longer.

'Why do you think?' he shot back gruffly. 'It's not something I generally like to shout about.'

She sighed. 'Okay, I get that it must have been humiliating and not an easy thing to talk about, but I could have done with knowing about it before coming here and having to find out about it from your friends.'

He took a step away and ran a hand through his hair, looking frustrated with himself. 'Yes, okay. You're right, I should have told you. I'm sorry.'

'It's fine. It's just – it makes it hard for me to react appropriately when I don't have all the information.' She frowned, not wanting to turn this into a fight, but determined to make her feelings very clear. 'I want to get this right, Xavier. For both our sakes.'

Xavier smiled back ruefully, his facial muscles tense. 'I appreciate that. I'll try to be a bit more open and honest with you from now on, I promise.'

'Thank you,' she said, giving him a nod of appreciation.

He looked back at her, his eyes seeming to grow darker as their gazes locked.

'You know, I'm really impressed with how you've handled yourself here today,' he murmured. 'I wasn't sure how it was going to go, but everyone we've spoken to has clearly really liked you.'

'That's probably because I asked them so many questions about themselves and actually listened to their answers,' she joked, a little uncomfortable with his praise.

'No. It's not just that. People really respond to you. You have a real charm about you and you're clearly very intelligent, judging by the way you followed the different conversations you were thrust into.'

She swallowed, feeling a bubble of pride rise through her chest. 'Thanks. That's really nice to hear. I've never thought of myself as intelligent.' She glanced away as heat began to creep up her neck. 'I wasn't great at learning at school – it bored me, to be honest – but I've read a lot since I've been working in the café, and I talk to such a wide variety of people in there every day I hear all sorts of interesting things. I guess it's made me good at general-knowledge subjects. In fact, I probably should warn you, I'm killer at Trivial Pursuit.'

He smiled at that and his whole face lit up.

Soli dragged in a breath as her body flooded with heat in response to it. He was such a beautiful man, even more so when he relaxed a little and let himself show his emotions on his face.

She swallowed as he took a step closer to her and reached out to pick a small leaf out of her hair. 'You look lovely today, by the way. I don't think I told you that back at the house. And I really appreciate you making so much effort for the party.'

'You're welcome,' she murmured through lips that were now having trouble forming actual words. He was standing so close to her, all she was aware of was his tantalising scent.

'We should probably slip away home now, before Veronica or Hugo come back out here,' he said, so quietly she was forced to lean in even closer to hear him. Her pulse throbbed hard in her veins as she felt the masculine heat of him radiate towards her. 'Veronica seemed intent on getting all the details about our marriage and I don't think I'm quite in the headspace to make up convincing enough lies right now,' he went on, apparently unaware of how he was turning her to jelly.

'Sure. Whatever you want,' she managed to say, forcing her frozen facial muscles into a smile.

Xavier was facing the house and he glanced towards it, seemingly to check if it was safe to make a sneaky exit, but he must have seen something, or someone, that alarmed him because the smile dropped from his face and his whole body stiffened. He appeared to pale as he continued to stare in shock at whatever had caught his attention.

'What's wrong?' Soli asked, turning to look in the direction he was gazing, a slow, heavy feeling of foreboding sinking through her.

'It's Harriet,' he replied in a tense voice.

'Your ex?' she asked, turning to watch a strikingly beautiful woman walking slowly towards them.

Soli frowned, wondering why she seemed to be moving so awkwardly, then as she looked down she realised the woman was heavily pregnant and the weight of the baby was making her waddle in her heels across the spongy grass.

'Yes,' was all Xavier had time to reply before Harriet was upon them, holding out her arms to Xavier in greeting.

'Xavier! I heard you were here with your new wife, so I thought it'd be all right to come over and say hello. It's wonderful to see you happy.' She offered Soli a friendly smile, the warmth in it only increasing her beauty. 'I'd heard you were becoming something of a confirmed bachelor-stroke-playboy.' She grinned affectionately at Xavier and Soli's stomach gave a sickening twist at how excluded she suddenly felt. These two clearly had some serious history between them.

And Harriet was exactly the sort of woman she'd expect Xavier to be married to. Elegant, intelligent and classically beautiful – the woman seemed to radiate vivacity. By stark contrast, Xavier's face looked stonier than ever.

'Oh, come on, Xave, you know I'm only teasing,' Harriet cooed, giving him a playful slap on the arm. This seemed to wake him up somehow and the corners of his mouth actually turned up for a moment. Not that the smile reached his eyes.

'I'm really happy for you,' he said in a voice that sounded as though he was having to force the words through his throat. 'You're actually glowing. I thought that was just an expression. I didn't realise pregnancy really did that to a woman.'

'So I've been told,' she said with a kind smile. 'It's all those hormones rushing around my system. I'm sure I won't look like this once the baby's born though. I've never been good with lack of sleep.'

'No. I remember,' Xavier said.

Soli's stomach twisted even harder, making her feel a bit sick. Now she was imagining the two of them in bed together, waking up and smiling at each other in mutual adoration before rolling together and—

No. Not going there right now.

'Well, I'd better get back to Neil – he'll be sending out a search party if I don't show myself soon. He's turned into something of a worrier since I fell pregnant. Calls me umpteen times a day to make sure I haven't gone into labour unexpectedly and forgotten to phone him!'

She shook her head, but from the way she was beaming, Soli could tell she didn't mind this show of over-the-top possessiveness one little bit.

She could understand that. It must be wonderful for someone to love and worry about you that much.

'When are you due?' she asked, to cover the slightly awkward atmosphere that throbbed between them all now.

'Three weeks. I can't wait, to be honest – I feel like an elephant lumbering around!'

She really didn't look like one though; she was carrying all at the front, so if you saw her from the back Soli bet you wouldn't even know she was pregnant.

'Oh, by the way,' she said, turning to Xavier, 'happy birthday for Wednesday. Are you doing anything special for it?' She glanced between the two of them with interest.

Soli tensed as an intense desire to protect Xavier from the hurt this woman had caused him mixed with a sting of her own hurt that he hadn't even mentioned his birthday to her.

'Yes, of course, but it's a big surprise,' she lied quickly, giving her a covert wink in the hope she'd believe the bluff. No way was she having this woman thinking she wasn't as good a partner to Xavier as Harriet had been in the past.

But then, Soli hadn't shredded his heart and humiliated him in front of the people he loved and respected most in the world, so she was already one up on her.

'Sweetheart, I'm so sorry to drag you away early but this migraine seems set to stay,' she said to Xavier, linking her fingers through his and feeling him squeeze her hand in silent thanks. 'It was good to meet you, Harriet. Good luck with the baby,' she said, giving the woman one last smile and a nod, then pulling subtly on Xavier's hand.

'Bye, Harriet,' Xavier said, falling into step with her as they walked back towards the house. They made a swift exit through the huge throng of people who were now milling around the large garden and made it back to the car without encountering any objections to their leaving.

'Thanks,' was all Xavier said as he pulled the car out of the parking space and set off back to their house.

Soli waited until they were driving down the main road into Hampstead before she asked, 'Are you okay?'

He didn't answer her immediately, just kept staring ahead at the road. 'Yeah, I'm fine,' he said eventually, though he really didn't sound it.

'I take it you didn't know she was pregnant?'

There was a heavy pause in which he stared at the road ahead again. 'No, I didn't.'

'How did it make you feel?' she asked tentatively.

He turned to glance at her and the expression in his eyes made her stomach sink to the floor. 'Not great, to be honest.' He dragged in a sharp breath. 'The main reason she gave for not wanting to marry me was that I wanted to have kids, but she didn't. She thought having a family would mean she wouldn't be able to focus on her career – that it'd hold her back.' His jaw clenched tight before he spoke again, as if he was fighting with his emotions. 'But I guess she did want kids after all – just not with me.'

Soli's stomach dropped even lower, making her feel nauseous on his behalf. 'Oh, Xavier, I'm so sorry.'

He shrugged. 'She probably had it right. I'd have been a terrible father and a selfish husband. I've been so focused on work and building my company I probably wouldn't have given my relationships priority – as I'm sure you've noticed,' he added with a grimace. There was a heavy pause before he cleared his throat and said, 'It was for the best that we didn't get married.'

She wanted to reassure him, to tell him that he had it all wrong, but she couldn't. She didn't know him well enough to be able to say something like that and he knew it.

Her heart went out to him. No wonder he was so unwilling to get close to someone again. Anybody would be wary of allowing themselves to love and trust if they'd been through what he had.

She wanted to help somehow, so much it made her chest physically ache.

But do what?

Taking a breath, she gave him a supportive smile as an idea began to form in her head.

She might not be able to do anything about the past, but she could definitely do something about the future.

Acknowledging a small but insistent voice in her head reminding her not to get too emotionally involved – because she knew, deep down, that if she set out on that path it would be almost impossible to turn back – she assured herself she would only do it to make their time together more enjoyable, and perhaps to say thank you to Xavier for giving her the chance to make a better life for herself and her family.

Yes. She would do it for him because she could.

But, perhaps even more importantly, because she knew that nobody else would.

9

MR & MRS – DISCOVER THINGS ABOUT YOUR PARTNER YOU DIDN'T KNOW.

It had been quite an eye-opener for Xavier, seeing Harriet for the first time in five years. The pregnancy had knocked him off his game to begin with, but once they'd started talking, he'd soon regained his equilibrium. Meeting her again had been something he'd been dreading, but now it had happened he realised it hadn't affected him in the way he'd expected.

In fact, he'd been surprised, after talking to Soli about it all and reflecting on it later that evening, by the startling realisation that he wasn't angry with Harriet any more, despite the pregnancy she'd sworn she'd never want. Thinking about what he'd had with her just conjured a sense of bittersweet nostalgia now, but that was all it was. It seemed he'd finally moved on from the hurt and bitterness he'd felt about her rejecting him.

It was actually quite liberating. He'd been walking around with this sense of loss and inadequacy for so long, it was a huge relief to finally feel it lifting.

He had a strong suspicion that Soli's steadfast support and compassion had had a hand in breaking the grief he'd been living with too. Her tackling the subject head-on had made him realise how he'd bottled his feelings up, and how unhealthy that had been. He'd not talked to anyone about what had happened to him before, worried it would make him seem weak, and had cut everyone who knew about it out of his life so that he hadn't had to face it. But he knew now he couldn't hide for ever. It was time to get past his hang-ups.

He had an inkling that Soli wouldn't let him carry on the way he'd been going anyway.

She was a real force of nature.

They'd spent the next day in the house together, with her reading a book in the garden and him moving between his home office and joining her on the terrace to eat, where they'd chatted about inconsequential things. He'd appreciated her allowing him some personal space and leaving the subject of Harriet alone, but also making it clear she was happy to talk if he wanted to.

It seemed he'd made a good move in choosing her to be his stand-in wife. He found he was actually enjoying her company now and could imagine them getting on fine for the next few months. Until it was time to call a halt to it all.

Strangely, the thought of that brought with it a heavy, tense feeling, so he pushed it to the back of his mind. There was no point in dwelling on what would happen when their arrangement came to an end. It was almost a year away yet.

* * *

Walking into the kitchen on the morning of his birthday to grab a quick cup of coffee, he stopped in amazement as he saw that the table was set for two and there was a plate loaded with Scotch pancakes covered in maple syrup and two large mugs of coffee sitting on it. Soli was standing at the stove, attending to what looked like poached eggs.

'Happy birthday!' she said brightly when she noticed him standing there, open-mouthed. 'I thought I'd make you breakfast. You like eggs, right?'

'Er... yes. I love them.'

'Great. Take a seat and dig in to the pancakes. I made them fresh. There's more coffee if you need a refill after that one too.'

'You didn't have to do this—' he began to protest, but she waved his words away.

'Of course I did! It's your birthday. Everyone should get special treatment on their birthday.'

Never having had 'special treatment' like this before, Xavier went to object, but snapped his mouth shut at the last second, feeling it would be rude and unkind to contradict her. Just because no one else had done it for him, it didn't mean he couldn't accept it from her. Tingly heat rushed across his skin as he made the conscious decision to accept her indulging him today. It would actually be pretty nice to celebrate his birthday. He'd not done it in a while.

'Well, I appreciate the thought,' he said, sitting down at the table. 'I'll wait for you before I eat though.'

'Okay,' she said, shooting him a warm smile.

A minute later, she came to join him, laying down plates of buttered wholemeal toast with two poached eggs balanced on top.

'So! What are you going to do with your day?' she asked, sitting down opposite him and picking up her cutlery.

He frowned at her. 'Go to work.'

She looked aghast. 'Really? Can't you take the day off for once?'

'I wasn't planning to. There's a lot going on at the minute.'

'But you have a large staff working for you.'

'Yes.'

'So let them do the work today. You're the boss, right? Take the day off and hang out with me. Treat yourself.'

He considered this for a moment, feeling a throb of unease about not going in to work at such short notice. Though, if he thought about it, he'd not had a day off in five years, so it was probably overdue. Soli was right too – his staff were more than capable of getting on with what needed doing without him for one day.

'Well, I suppose I could—'

'Great!' She grinned at this and began tucking into her breakfast.

After they'd finished the delicious meal, Soli ordered him to go and sit in the garden and read the papers that she'd nipped out and bought earlier while she cleared up. She wouldn't hear of him helping her, even though he pointed out he should be the one to do it since she'd cooked.

They spent a lovely morning looking out across the garden, reading and chatting about current affairs, which she seemed impressively clued up on – another by-product of working in the cafe, he supposed.

Just before lunchtime, Soli stood up and brushed down her skirt. 'Right! It's time for a walk on the heath, then lunch. I've already put together a picnic. You'll need your swimming trunks, your trainers and your tennis racket,' she called over her shoulder, as she walked away into the house.

He stared after her, dumbstruck, his body rushing with endorphins, as it occurred to him what she'd done. She'd planned the 'perfect day' he'd told her about for his birthday.

Heat pooled in his belly, and he was horrified to find his eyes had welled with tears.

No. No! He couldn't allow himself to feel sentimental about this. She was just fulfilling some obligation she felt she had as his wife, that was all.

Still, a little voice told him, she hadn't needed to do it, and from the glee he'd heard in her voice he suspected she was actually enjoying it.

* * *

A couple of hours later they were stretched out on picnic blankets, groaning happily after wolfing down the fabulous lunch she'd put together, which included slices of her amazing – and apparently legendary – chocolate fudge cake.

'I can see why that's so popular in your cafe,' Xavier said, nodding towards the now empty container that had held the cake. 'I don't think I've ever tasted anything like it.'

'An "orgasm in food form", one of my friends calls it,' she said with a grin.

There was a small pause, where they didn't look at each other for a moment and pretended to watch a couple of squirrels running up a tree trunk instead.

Xavier cleared his throat, reminding himself what a bad idea it would be to act on the kinds of thoughts that had just popped into his head following that comment.

'So, tell me what your perfect day would consist of,' he said, attempting to circumnavigate the strange atmosphere now zinging between them.

Her brow furrowed as she appeared to think about this for a moment.

'Well, if I could choose anything, I'd probably go for spending the day on a Mediterranean island. I'd eat lunch on the beach and go for a swim in the sea. Then I'd spend the evening having someone servicing my every need.'

'That sounds good,' he said, smiling at her and noticing how her cheeks had flushed an adorable shade of pink. 'I think I could probably manage to enjoy a day like that too.'

'Well, maybe we'll do it for your next birthday,' she quipped, her face falling as it obviously occurred to her that they wouldn't be together for his next birthday. Their time, and their marriage, would be over by then.

'When was the last time you had a holiday abroad?' he asked hurriedly, attempting to sweep past the awkwardness.

'Er...' She thought about this for a second, looking relieved to have the conversational diversion.

'I guess it was about four years ago, just before my dad died. We went to Brittany on the ferry. It was a great holiday. We were all really happy.' He saw grief flash across her face and a sudden and acute instinct to make her happy again overwhelmed him.

'You know, it's probably been that long for me too. I've been so focused on building the business, I've not stopped to take a proper break.' He dragged in a breath, throwing caution to the wind. 'You know, I own a holiday property on Corsica. It's just been renovated, and they've completed the fit-out early, so it's just sitting empty at the moment. We could go and stay for a week.' He shrugged, trying to appear nonchalant. 'It would do us both good to get away.' He smiled. 'And there wouldn't be any solicitors there, checking up on us.'

Her eyes had lit with excitement as he'd talked and as soon as he finished speaking, she blurted, 'That would be amazing! I've always wanted to go there. It sounds like such a beautiful place.'

'Okay, then,' he said, satisfaction coursing through him at being able to bring back her smile. 'I'll arrange for us to go this Saturday. I'll just need to let my colleagues know.' He paused and smiled to himself. 'They're going to wonder what's happened to me. I never take time off.'

'I guess they'll just assume you're having a honeymoon with your new wife,' she pointed out with a grin.

'Yes, of course.' He blinked, realising it was a detail he'd overlooked and feeling pleased it would still fit their story. That solidified it as a really good practical excuse to go.

Satisfied with his decision, he lay back and stared up at the fluffy clouds floating slowly across the sky above him.

Yes. Getting some sun on their faces, eating good food and relaxing would be a great thing for both of them.

* * *

Soli's stomach had jumped with excitement as they'd stepped off the plane that Xavier had chartered, into the balmy Corsican air. She'd not been able to believe it when he'd led them to a private lounge at the airport and announced in a really matter-of-fact voice that their pilot would be there to greet them soon and they would be in Corsica within a couple of hours.

Soli's only experience of being on a plane had been on a family holiday to Spain when they'd gone with a budget airline. This trip had been entirely different, what with the separate leather seats, à la carte food and total lack of general public.

And then when he'd led them over to a soft-top classic car and loaded their bags into the boot, her insides had done a little dance of excitement. The trip to his hillside house had been a thing of joy.

The cliff-top cottage where they were to stay for the next week was quite a bit smaller than the Hampstead house, but no less impressive. It had been newly decorated in fresh Mediterranean colours and filled with French-style furniture, all of which looked incredibly expensive and dauntingly classy.

'It's a rental aimed at the high-end market,' Xavier said conversationally as they walked inside, and Soli gasped in delight at the amazing view of the sea through panoramic bifolding doors. 'We have our own private cove down there,' he said, walking to the doors and opening them back so the sweet, briny smell of the sea below them rushed inside and tickled her nose.

'It's a bit of a walk down a narrow path in the cliff, but well worth it.'

Soli followed him onto the deck, which housed a couple of comfortable-looking loungers as well as a small dining table with a canopy flapping gently in the warm breeze, and turned to give him a smile that felt as if it might split her face in two. 'I love it!' she said, her voice raspy with delight. 'I can't wait to explore.'

'Let me show you your room first,' he said, strolling back inside.

She followed him through the living area and down a short corridor to where two doors stood opposite each other.

'You're in here,' he said, opening the door on the right. They walked inside and stood by the king-sized bed that was dressed with white linen sheets and an abundance of pillows in a soft blue-grey colour.

'There's an en-suite bathroom over there,' he said, gesturing to a small door on the right.

'Oh, Xavier, it's wonderful!' she said, turning to give him a grateful smile. It was a long time since she'd been this excited about being somewhere and her whole body felt jittery with adrenaline. Or was it that she was nervous about being here with him? The whole place shouted *Romance!*

He smiled back at her with the genuine, wide grin that always made her tummy flutter whenever he decided to trust her with it. 'I'm glad you like it.' He huffed out a breath, frowning down at the floor before looking back into her eyes. 'I wanted to say thank you – for all the support you've given me recently. It was above and beyond the call of duty and I want you to know I really appreciate it.'

She suddenly felt a bit shy. 'It was my pleasure. Anything to help.'

The air between them felt prickly with emotion. Or was she imagining it?

Something in his expression made her breath catch in her throat.

'You know, you're the most genuinely caring person I've ever met,' he murmured, taking a step closer to her.

Soli was suddenly intensely aware of how alone the two of them were, and how close to the enormous, inviting bed.

Heat throbbed through her, making her head swim.

'Thank you,' she breathed through numbed lips. She suddenly wanted to kiss him so badly her whole body ached with it.

The look in his eyes mesmerised her, keeping her suspended in a state of such intense longing she knew she had no hope of escaping from it. It wouldn't take much to be close enough to touch him. Just one more step. She could feel the heat radiating from his body and his enticing scent filled her nose, making her mouth water.

His Adam's apple bobbed in his throat as he swallowed, and her gaze flashed down to it for a second.

The break in eye contact seemed to shock him out of whatever state he was in, and he gave a rough cough and took a step backwards, sweeping his hand towards the door.

'Okay, well, I'll grab the bags from the car and you can get settled in. We should go out for dinner. There's a lovely tavern in the next town with magnificent views of the harbour. It's quite a sight.'

It was as if he'd brought the shutters down on his emotions.

'That sounds wonderful,' Soli said quietly, her stomach sinking with disappointment at his sudden change in demeanour.

'Good,' he said, giving her a jerky nod and swiftly leaving the room.

She flopped down onto the bed and took a few deep, steadying breaths.

Perhaps this holiday wasn't going to be as relaxing as she'd hoped.

* * *

The tavern was as magnificent as Xavier had described and Soli had a hard time choosing what to eat from the comprehensive seafood menu.

'I don't usually eat fish. I've never learnt to cook it because Domino has an extreme aversion to the smell,' she said, her mouth watering at the thought of the meal she'd just ordered. She'd been hesitant to ask for the lobster – she'd always wanted to try it – but Xavier seemed to have sensed her worry and told her to order whatever she wanted. So lobster it was, with a large glass of crisp Sancerre, which he'd recommended.

She was in heaven.

'So, I thought tomorrow we could explore some of the coves. Maybe take a picnic lunch with us. I have a small motorboat moored in our cove which we can take along the coast,' Xavier said, putting down his wine glass and fixing her with his tingle-inducing gaze.

'Oh, wow! I'd love that!' she said. This whole set-up was like something from the movies.

The smile he gave her made his eyes twinkle and she took a hurried gulp of her own wine to calm her suddenly racing pulse.

She needed to remember that this wasn't real. They were just pretending.

At least he was.

She wasn't so sure about herself any more.

* * *

They slept in late the next morning on Xavier's insistence and ate a light breakfast before strolling down the winding path to their cove and climbing into the boat.

The turquoise sea glittered in the late morning sunlight and Soli laughed with joy as they sped through the gentle waves to the other side of the island and one of the other secluded, and usually deserted, coves that Xavier knew about.

Once there, he brought the boat in to shore and tied it to a large rock, making sure it wouldn't float away before helping Soli out. Her hand was warm and firm in his and for a moment he contemplated not letting go of her and pulling her towards him instead.

To do what, he wasn't sure.

No. He was. But he couldn't allow himself to think like that. They'd made a pact and he needed to keep to it. For his own sanity.

After exploring the small cove, where Soli scrambled over the rocks and stood on the largest one with her hands on her hips and her curls blowing in the wind – eliciting in him the strangest feeling of lightness he'd ever experienced – they settled down onto the picnic blanket he'd brought and tucked into the food his housekeeper had stocked the fridge with.

Once they'd finished, he lay back on the blanket with his hands behind his head and gazed up at the azure-blue sky, letting the heat of the day wash over him. It had been a very long time since he'd felt this relaxed – even though an undercurrent of crackling energy still pulsed through him. Something he couldn't quite identify, though he had his suspicions.

'Phew! It's so hot!' Soli said next to him. 'I think I'll go for a swim. Want to join me?' She looked at him expectantly.

'Not right now,' he said, unwilling to move from his comfortable position. 'You go ahead.'

He tried not to watch as she took off the light summer dress she'd been wearing to uncover a cherry-red bikini.

Tried and failed.

He also tried to keep his gaze off her as she skipped down the golden sand to the water and tentatively dipped her toes in.

That was a lost hope too.

'It's warm,' she called back, sounding delighted with the discovery.

He gave up and turned to rest on his side, watching her splash around, grinning from ear to ear as she went deeper into the water.

Her body was lithe, but curvaceous, imperfect in places – and wonderfully real for it.

It had to be the most alluring sight he'd ever seen.

She was magnificent, standing tall and proud in the waves as they gently lapped at her thighs. The very picture of female beauty.

A sense of contentment washed over him, taking him by surprise.

Being here with Soli felt so very right.

He was both amazed and pleased by how much he'd found he enjoyed sharing things with her. Being an only child, he wasn't used to sharing, so he was surprised to find how much he actually liked it. Soli took such joy in being introduced to new things too and she seemed to genuinely enjoy them. The women he usually dated were well used to the high life and didn't tend to comment much on the places he took them or the gifts he bought, so it had been wonderful to see Soli's genuine appreciation. It made him feel as though he was making a valuable contribution to her happiness, and her life. Something he'd never experienced before with a partner.

She was so full of wonder and enchantment with the world, despite the trials she'd been through in her life.

He'd never met such a positive person and it thrilled him to his core.

What was he doing, anyway, just lying there alone? He should take her lead and go and enjoy himself in the water.

With her.

Pushing himself up to standing, he walked swiftly across the hot sand, feeling acute pleasure as the cool sea rushed over his feet and lapped against his legs. He waded towards where she was bobbing about in the water and when she turned and saw him coming her face broke into a smile.

Euphoria swelled in the pit of his stomach, then rushed up through his chest, taking his breath away.

'The water feels incredible against your hot skin,' she called, moving forwards to meet him.

All he could think about at that moment was what it would feel like to touch her slick skin and feel her incredible body pressed against him.

Her smile faltered as he got closer and he realised that the longing he was feeling must be showing on his face.

'Are you okay?' she asked, reaching out to him and putting her hand on his shoulder. Before he knew what was happening a particularly strong wave had pushed her towards him and their bodies connected, their mouths only inches apart now. The feeling of her pressed against him tipped him over the edge and without another thought he dropped his mouth to hers, sliding his hands around her waist to steady them both.

Everything else faded away as the sensation of her soft lips under his took over his entire awareness, plunging him into a state of desire so intense it left him breathless. Instinctively he deepened the kiss and felt her respond, opening her mouth so he could slide his tongue inside. She tasted just as sweet as he remembered, but also salty from the seawater, and he let out a groan of pleasure deep in his throat. Her body was slippery and smooth against his and he pulled her closer to him, losing himself in pure physical indulgence.

He'd wanted to do this for so damn long.

His body responded as his desire deepened, hardening and pressing into her with obvious intent.

'Oh!' she gasped against his mouth and the sound of her surprise shocked him out of his erotic daze. He pulled away abruptly, suddenly furious with himself for allowing his need to override his common sense. What was he doing? He couldn't kiss her like this and expect everything to stay the same between them.

But did he really want it to?

Yes. They couldn't afford to let their agreement slip; it wasn't sensible.

'Sorry,' he muttered, drawing away from her and noting with a sting of regret how shell-shocked she seemed by his sudden withdrawal. 'I shouldn't have done that.'

'No. Okay,' she rasped, her confusion clear on her face.

'I'm going for a swim, then we should think about getting back to the house,' he said gruffly, diving underneath the cool water before she had a chance to answer him, praying it would bring him back to his senses and extinguish his driving need to swim right back and kiss her again.

* * *

'You know, you're very mature for your age. I guess that comes from taking on so much responsibility when you were so young,' he said to her later, back at the house, while they sat on the terrace gazing out over the water, sipping their second large glasses of wine, trying to pretend that the kiss hadn't really happened.

She turned to shoot him a startled smile. 'Do you think so? Most of the time I feel like I have no idea how to be an adult.'

He gave her a wry smile back. 'I think most people feel like that. We're all just making it up as we go along.'

'That's good to hear.'

There was a small pause where they just looked at each other.

'I'm... er... just going to get a glass of water. This wine's going straight to my head,' she said, standing up quickly and stumbling as she caught her foot on the chair leg.

Xavier shot out a hand to steady her, rising from his chair so he could take her weight.

She gazed up into his eyes, an expression of embarrassment clouding her face. 'Sorry,' she whispered.

'No need to be sorry,' he said roughly, hyper-aware of his pulse throbbing in his throat. She smelt wonderful, like sunshine and fresh air and her own distinctive sweetness, and he drew in a great lungful of her scent, his chest swelling with a longing so powerful his whole body rushed with it.

'Soli...' He wasn't sure what he wanted to say. A thousand thoughts flashed through his head, but words wouldn't form in his mouth.

So he kissed her again. Hard.

She let out a small gasp of surprise, but didn't pull away. Instead she wrapped her arms around his back and pulled him closer to her, forcing their bodies together.

And then his hands were in her hair, and his body was responding in all sorts of inappropriate ways, but he couldn't stop himself this time. Didn't want to.

From the desperate sounds in her throat, it seemed as though Soli was having the exact same problem.

'Let's go inside,' she murmured when he pulled back a fraction to breathe, her grip tightening on him as if she was afraid he might change his mind again and let her go.

Through his haze of desire, Xavier couldn't remember any of the reasons why they should stop any more, so without another word he slid his hands beneath her thighs and lifted her up against him and carried her into the house, still kissing her as he went, unwilling to break the connection.

In the bedroom they discarded their clothes quickly and he rolled on top of her, luxuriating in the feeling of her soft skin against his.

Through the fug of feeling, a terrible thought struck him like a blow. 'I don't have any condoms,' he bit out, suddenly furious with himself for overlooking such a simple thing. His thoughts swirled wildly as he tried to reconcile all the concerns that were now jabbing at the edges of his brain.

'It's okay, I'm on the pill,' she muttered back, gazing up into his eyes with a look of such genuine honesty he knew deep down that she was telling him the truth. Because she always told him the truth.

'Thank God for that,' he said, letting out a breath and feeling relief radiate from the pit of his stomach. Sliding his hands back into her hair, he took a moment to marvel at the sensation of the silky strands running through his fingers. 'Thank God,' he repeated huskily, before losing himself in the wonderfulness of her again.

10

DOMINOES – SET THEM UP WITH A STEADY HAND, THEN SEE THEM FALL WITH THE SLIGHTEST KNOCK.

Xavier sat on the terrace cradling a large cup of coffee in his hands and staring out over the sea as the sun rose in the distance.

He'd left Soli sleeping peacefully in his bed, with her wild curls spread out around her head. He'd had to force himself to leave the room and not slide back in next to her and pull her soft, welcoming body against him again.

What the hell did he think he was doing, messing with their no-sex agreement like that? All day yesterday he'd fought the urge to get closer to her, keeping his physical distance and his tone light and friendly. He'd deliberately not flirted in any way, strictly disciplining himself against giving in to the desire that had swelled and throbbed inside him.

And then it had all gone to hell.

It had been the heady mixture of sunshine and lust and then being forced to touch her again when she'd stumbled that had been his final undoing. The expression of open hunger in her eyes when she'd looked up at him had been impossible to resist.

The sex had been great too. Fun and surprising in its intensity. They'd fitted together so well, delighting in exploring each other's bodies for the first time but also seeming to know intuitively what made the other tick.

They had been around each other a lot recently, of course, so maybe that was why it had felt so comfortable being with her.

Not that he was going to let it happen again. No. He'd be a fool to indulge his base desires and potentially ruin the good thing they had going. The last thing he needed was for this business relationship to take a wrong turn and for the solicitors to get wind and it put his inheritance in jeopardy.

That house was much more important to him than sating his physical desires for the next few months.

When Soli got up, he'd discuss that with her in a straight and honest manner. He didn't want her to think he'd taken advantage of her last night, but he wanted to make it clear that it had been a mistake on his part and that they should move their relationship back to one of friendship only.

Surely, she'd understand the necessity of that. She might even wake up this morning regretting what had happened last night too.

Just as he thought this there was movement by the terrace doors and Soli emerged into the sunlight wearing one of the robes from the room.

He swallowed hard and gave her a friendly but controlled smile, not wanting to make her feel awkward, but needing to set the right business-like tone for the conversation that was to come.

'Good morning,' he said as she moved slowly towards him, appearing to stumble a little on the smooth tiled floor. 'Are you okay?' he asked, feeling a sting of concern as she got closer to him.

She really didn't look good. Her skin was a strange grey-green colour, and her eyes looked a little unfocused.

'I don't feel too great actually.'

'Here.' He stood up and pulled out a chair for her. 'Sit down.'

She came towards him and put her hand on the back of the chair, as if not entirely convinced it was what she wanted to do.

'I felt a bit light-headed last night, but I thought it was because of the... um... wine.'

And the sexual tension, he filled in silently for her.

There was a sudden flash of panic in her eyes and she took a hasty step backwards. 'Sorry. Excuse me for a second—' and with that, she dashed back inside, the door to her bedroom slamming loudly behind her.

Panic inched through him. He had no idea what he should do. Should he go into the bedroom to check if she was okay? If she was being sick she might prefer that he leave her alone. Or was she hoping he'd go in there and hold her hair and rub her back? No. He couldn't imagine her wanting that. Especially with their relationship being so... confused right now. So, he stayed at the table and waited, with his pulse beating hard in his head, until he heard her bedroom door open again.

Striding into the living area, he saw her standing in the doorway, seemingly holding herself up by propping her hands against the door jambs.

'You should go straight back to bed,' he said, noting how she was trembling now.

'I don't think I drank too much last night, I think I'm ill,' she murmured, looking at him with bloodshot eyes. 'I must have picked up a tummy bug from somewhere, or perhaps it was something I ate—'

'I agree. Straight back to bed for you.' She nodded and turned around, heading back into her room, where she climbed shakily under the fresh cotton sheets of her bed.

Good that we used my bed last night, so her sheets are clean, he thought as she snuggled into the pillows and let out a small sigh of relief. At least she'd be able to lie there without being constantly reminded of what happened between them last night. He didn't want her associating it with feeling ill.

Not that that should be his priority right now, he reminded himself sternly. 'I'll go and fetch you a glass of water,' he said, heading quickly out of the room and into the kitchen.

He filled a glass for her and searched out a bowl from the cleaning cupboard, which he then took into her bedroom.

'Here you go, just in case you feel ill again and don't think you can make it to the bathroom. Not that it'll be a problem,' he added quickly, not wanting her to think he'd be angry if she made a mess.

'Thank you,' she whispered, clearly trying to smile at him, but not quite managing it.

'Try and sleep,' he said quietly, backing out of the room. 'If you need me, shout. I'll be right next door.'

He saw her give him a small nod before he turned around and headed back to the living area.

It looked as if the conversation about what had happened last night was going to have to wait.

* * *

Soli slept fitfully, weaving in and out of consciousness, sometimes aware of Xavier's presence in the room, other times thinking she must have imagined it.

In the middle of the night, she rolled over and stretched out her arm to see whether he'd got into bed with her, but had found the other side cold and empty.

Not that she could blame him. Who'd want to sleep next to someone who had to get up to vomit every half an hour? She hoped to goodness he wasn't sick too – that would really make her feel wretched. He'd been really kind, looking after her, coming in to check on her regularly and refreshing her water. Luckily, she'd not needed the bowl he'd brought in. The thought of him having to deal with that had given her the horrors.

She couldn't bring herself to think about what had happened between them the night before though. As wonderful as it had been, it made her stomach tie into knots just thinking about it, so she pushed it to the back of her mind. It would be something she'd mull over once she was feeling better – which would hopefully be soon.

She hated being ill.

Especially when she was meant to be on holiday.

And with Xavier right next door.

* * *

She was still sick the following day and only got out of bed to dry heave before crawling back under the covers to sleep, but the morning after that she woke up feeling as if the worst of it had lifted and tentatively sat up in bed to check the time.

Ten o'clock.

She'd been in bed for nearly two days.

Poor Xavier – he must have been bored out of his mind.

Slowly, carefully, she swung her legs out of bed and tested how she'd feel standing up, finding she wasn't as dizzy as she'd been the day before, and instead of lurching, her stomach gave a growl of hunger.

Thank goodness for that.

It seemed it was only a forty-eight-hour bug. Still, as she pulled on her robe and made her way to the door she had a moment where she thought she might pass out.

Better take it easy, Soli; no need to rush.

After pressing her hands to the wall and taking a few deep breaths to give her head a chance to catch up with the movement, she walked slowly out of the room and into the living area.

It appeared to be deserted, though there was a smell of coffee in the air and a plate and a mug next to the sink.

'How are you feeling this morning?' came a voice from outside and she turned to see that Xavier was sitting on the terrace, looking at her with concern in his eyes.

'A lot better, thanks,' she said, walking slowly out onto the terrace and over to where he was sitting on one of the loungers with a tablet on his lap.

'You still look a bit pale. Are you sure you're okay to be up?' he asked, his gaze raking her face.

She cursed herself for not even looking in the mirror and flattening down her hair before leaving her room, but decided just to brazen it out now she was here. He certainly didn't look disgusted by her appearance. If anything, his expression was one of friendly concern.

'A bit of fresh air will probably do me the world of good,' she said, sitting down carefully on the lounger next to him and offering him a tentative smile. 'I'm so sorry for ruining your holiday.'

He waved a hand at her. 'Don't be ridiculous. It's not as if you got ill on purpose.' He sat up and swung his legs to the side, putting the tablet onto a coffee table next to him. 'Could you eat?'

'Actually, yes. I think I could.'

He nodded. 'Okay. Stay there. I'll fetch you some breakfast.'

Before she could object, he stood up and strode swiftly and purposefully back into the house, returning a few minutes later with a mug of coffee and a plate of wholemeal toast.

'Here,' he said, handing her the food, then putting the drink onto the table next to his tablet. 'I thought something quite plain would be good to start with.'

'Thank you,' she said, gratefully accepting the plate and sitting up on the lounger to eat.

She felt him watching her as she took her first tentative bite, then when it was obvious she wasn't going to be sick again he went back into the house, returning a couple of minutes later with a mug of coffee for himself.

'I guess you were hungry,' he said, gesturing to the now empty plate she had on her lap.

'I guess I was,' she agreed, giving him a grateful smile.

'Listen. We don't need to rush off anywhere today, if you're worried about that,' he said, his expression sincere. 'I'll be very happy to hang out here until you feel more up to going out. Perhaps you could teach me how to play a board game or something.'

'That would be great,' she said, immediately perking up at the thought. Lazing around and recuperating whilst playing one of her favourite games would be her idea of heaven right now. 'Except I didn't bring one with me.'

'No problem,' Xavier said with a twitch of his eyebrows. 'We have some here in the house. Apparently, they're popular with holidaymakers who want to switch off their phones and get back to a screen-free existence for the duration of their stay, or so the interior designer told me the other day. It made me think of you actually.'

She blinked in surprise. 'Well, that's great. I guess the lure of board games isn't dead after all.'

'I guess not,' he agreed, the corner of his mouth turning up. 'I'll go and fetch them and we can have a game now if you feel up to it.'

'Great,' she said, 'but we should move to the table. I take my playing very seriously.'

'I'd expect nothing less,' he said with a smile.

So he went to the fetch the games that he'd had stocked in a cupboard in the living area for guests – as a reaction to her love for them? she wondered hopefully – while she went to get dressed.

They played happily for the next couple of hours, sipping coffee and feeling the warm sea breeze on their faces as they alternated between asking questions and answering them, each taking great pleasure in challenging the other's knowledge of random facts.

'I really appreciate you looking after me. It's kind of you,' Soli said after they'd finally called a halt to the game. She'd been intensely aware of all the things they hadn't said to each other since 'the other night' and wanted to clear the air so she could breathe properly again. Even if it meant dealing with something she didn't want to hear. Which, from Xavier's careful avoidance of touching her or maintaining eye contact for too long, she suspected might be that he believed they'd made a mistake in sleeping together.

Nausea rose from her stomach as she waited for his response, only this time it came about through nerves.

'Well, I did agree to be there for you in sickness and in health, so I guess I'm just fulfilling my promise,' he quipped, though she couldn't help but notice how his whole body had tensed.

She shot him a sheepish smile. 'Still, it's good of you.'

He shrugged, clearly uncomfortable with her praising him. 'You deserve to be looked after too,' he said gruffly.

Letting out a low breath, she leant back in her chair and crossed her arms. 'I guess I'm just not used to it any more. It's been a while.'

'Since your dad died?' he asked, their gazes locking.

The sudden swell of emotion she experienced made her suck in a breath.

'Yeah,' she said, telling herself to pull it together. This was no time to go to pieces.

Xavier seemed to sense her discomfort and gave her an understanding nod. 'Hey, I forgot to ask – how's your sister doing at Oxford?'

'Great! It sounds like she's really enjoying herself,' she said, grateful for the change in conversation.

'Good for you for making that happen. I'm seriously impressed. I'm not sure many siblings would go to the lengths you did to make sure their sister was set up like that.'

She shrugged, but her face heated at the compliment. 'It would have been a crime not to let her go to university. She's so smart. The world is going to thank me one day.'

'I'm sure it is.' He sat back and studied her for a moment. 'I guess I should thank you too. You saved me from losing my home. And perhaps my sanity.' His smile was wry.

'Well, you've been very generous. You've given me more than I asked for.'

He laughed, perhaps to cover his unease. 'We seem to have turned into the Mutual Admiration Society.'

She smiled. 'Yes, I guess we have.'

'Well, why not? We are pretty amazing people, are we not?'

'We are, I suppose.'

'No! No "suppose" about it. We are.'

Their gazes locked and Soli got lost in a sudden flash of memory as she thought of how he'd looked into her eyes while they were making love.

'Listen. About what happened the other night,' he said in a careful tone that made her spirits plummet.

'Yes?'

'I don't think it's a good idea to let that happen again. Especially since we still have rather a long time to live together. It could make things tricky.' He didn't say, 'if we end up falling out,' but it was implicit in his manner.

'Oh. Er... okay.' She tried not to sound disappointed, but obviously failed because he said, 'It's for the best, Soli,' in a tone that brooked no argument.

'I'm not looking for you to fall in love with me or anything, you know,' she said without stopping to think too hard about what she was saying. 'We could keep it as a purely physical thing. No strings.'

'I'm not sure those arrangements ever work,' he said, his expression radiating extreme scepticism.

Even though her brain was telling her he might have a point, her libido didn't want to listen. They'd crossed the line now and there was no real way back, it pointed out. In fact, it actually felt to her as if she'd turned a corner in her life after sleeping with Xavier – that she'd finally stepped into adulthood. Now she'd pushed herself over the ledge and found her heart had survived it, she was confident she was mature enough to keep sex and love separate.

'We'd make it work. We both know we're not in this for the long haul. It's just temporary. And it'd make living together much more fun and much less frustrating.' She flashed him a smile, which he returned. 'Especially since we agreed not to see other people during the time we're married,' she added.

There was a short pause while he appeared to consider this.

'No. I don't think it's a good idea,' he said eventually, and she could tell from the resolute look in his eyes that he'd made his mind up and was unlikely to change it.

The businessman was back.

Her heart sank.

'Okay, whatever you think,' she said brightly to cover her frustration. Perhaps he was right. It might make things more complicated.

But it didn't stop her from hoping he'd change his mind.

* * *

The journey home was just as luxurious and comfortable as the one out there, except for a strange sort of stiffness between them that hadn't been there previously. They'd been really careful around each other ever since they'd had that conversation about not having sex again, as if they were tiptoeing around a bombshell that could trigger the second they relaxed and took a misstep, and it was making both of them act in an over-the-top, super-polite way towards each other.

So by the time they walked in through the front door to the Hampstead house, Soli was completely and utterly exhausted from nervous tension.

So much for having a relaxing holiday.

Xavier immediately excused himself and she found herself alone again in the kitchen, fixing herself a meal for one, wondering whether her life would ever be normal again.

She came to the conclusion that it was very unlikely. Especially now she knew how wonderful it could be to be wanted by Xavier McQueen. She'd so enjoyed being able to get close to him. They'd been good together in bed. He was certainly a lot better than the men – well, boys really – that she'd slept with in the past. He'd known exactly what to do to give her the most pleasure and had been incredibly attentive to her needs. She'd never experienced anything like it. And she wanted more. Much more.

The idea of living with him until the year was up, with this sexual tension throbbing between them the whole time, and not being allowed to act on it, made her stomach turn over with restlessness. They'd go insane, surely.

They'd be much better to give in to their physical urges and ride things out till the marriage was up. They'd probably be bored with each other by then anyway.

Refusing to listen to a niggling little voice that told her not to bank on that, she decided to keep herself open to the chance it could happen, but not push for it in any way. Xavier was definitely the kind of man who needed to feel in control of his decisions – and his destiny – so if it was going to happen it would need to come from him.

It would be fine with her either way.

Absolutely fine.

To keep herself occupied, so she wouldn't go crazy thinking about it all day, she went to see her mum, who seemed to be getting on well with the carer, then went into the cafe to check everything had run smoothly without her.

After being away for a while she found, to her shock and distress, that the place seemed shabby and cluttered to her now, and the warm, cosy atmosphere, that she'd been using as the excuse not to change a thing about it, was sadly lacking. It had all been in her head. A phantom of the past.

She'd been desperately hanging on to her father's vision for the place, to try and keep a part of him alive, but it was actually holding the business back. Destroying it, in fact.

He never would have wanted that.

She knew now, with absolute clarity, that it was time to let go. She needed to stop being afraid of the future and allow herself to finally move on.

It was time to make some changes.

* * *

It took two more days of Xavier making himself scarce in the evenings and acting all stiff and formal with her again before Soli's resolve to be cool and indifferent about how their relationship would go from now on snapped.

'Are we really back to you treating me like a piece of furniture again?' she bit out in frustration the morning of the third day, when Xavier swept into the kitchen, poured himself a coffee and gave her a polite nod before starting to retreat outside with it.

He turned back, then carefully put his mug down on the nearest work surface, the coffee slopping over the edge as if his hand had been trembling.

'That's not what I'm doing, Soli,' he said quietly, his expression surprisingly tortured.

Her stomach flipped at the sight of it, but she held her nerve. They really needed to address this and the sooner the better.

'Look, I get that you don't want to have a physical relationship with me, but I'd really prefer it if you at least acknowledged my presence in the house. We can be friends, surely?'

The muscle in his jaw was working overtime. 'It's not that I don't want a physical relationship with you,' he ground out, taking a step towards her, his shoulders rigid and his eyes flashing with frustration, 'it's that I do.'

'You do?' she whispered, shocked by the passion in his voice and the intensity in his eyes.

'Yes,' he said, letting out a low, frustrated-sounding breath.

'Oh. Okay. I see.'

'And seeing you every day but not being able to touch you, when I know how good we can be together, is driving me insane.' His chest rose and fell in rapid movements as if he was fighting for control and barely keeping it together.

The idea that she was doing that to him thrilled her to her core. Without thinking, she took a step closer to him, unable to fight the instinct to push him a little bit further to see what he'd do.

They stared into each other's eyes, their breath coming fast and their bodies tense.

Xavier made the first move, closing the gap between them and sliding his hand into her hair, then pulling her towards him so her mouth met his. The kiss was rough and full of the longing they'd both been battling since the last time they'd given in to the need to touch each other.

He let out a low growl in the base of his throat as she wound her arms around him and pressed herself closer to him, feeling exactly how much he wanted her right then.

She pulled back from the kiss to look him in the eyes again, wanting to make sure they were both thinking the same way before this went any further, so they didn't end up in an even more awkward position later.

'I thought you said—'

'I know what I said, but I decided not to listen to myself for once,' he ground out, his brow pinched in a half-relieved, half-frustrated sort of frown. His eyes were alive with pleasure though, which her body responded to by sending a throb of pure desire through her.

She couldn't help but grin at him. 'Good decision. Let's be wild. It's a healthy life choice.'

'I don't know about healthy...' His words tickled her lips.

'Liberating, then. We're grown-ups. We can handle it. Both of us know the score and we're not looking for anything in addition to our agreement.'

'You mean that, right?' His expression was deadly serious now.

'Yes,' she said, matching his seriousness with her own. 'I absolutely do. I promise.'

His hands had been tight on her back, holding her against him, but they relaxed a little as something seemed to occur to him. 'Still, we need to be sensible, so we should use condoms too from now on, just to be extra-safe,' he said.

She nodded. 'Fine by me.'

And it was fine, because the last thing she needed right now was an added complication in her life.

11

BATTLESHIPS – SINK YOUR OPPONENT WITH A BLOW TO THE HEART.

Xavier was late for work, for the first time ever, after taking Soli to bed then having a lot of trouble forcing himself to get out of it again and leave her there, all warm and sexily rumpled.

It had definitely been worth it though. More than worth it. All the pent-up frustration and jagged need that had been stressing him out – to the point where he was having trouble concentrating at work – completely evaporated the moment he let himself give in and do what he'd been desperate to do again ever since that incredible night in Corsica.

Ever since they'd crossed that line it had been inevitable they wouldn't be able to go back to their platonic existence.

He felt pretty confident it would be okay though. They'd had another talk about sex not changing anything about their deal and had both agreed they were still happy with that. Their physical relationship would only last as long as the marriage; after that they'd both walk away.

A clean break.

Now the thought of having Soli at home, waiting for him every evening, had a very different impact on his mood.

He even started coming home from work earlier, looking forward to spending his evenings with her, eating her wonderful food, or seeing the look of astonished approval when he insisted on cooking for her instead.

Life was pleasingly satisfying and straightforward, with his rapport with Soli on an even keel, both knowing exactly where they stood with each other.

There was no pretence and no underlying conflict of interest.

It was the most simple and rewarding relationship he'd ever had.

She seemed to know just how to pull him out of one of his funks with a few choice words and a smile, and she charmed him with her positivity and humble joy. For those few weeks he felt as if he was finally living the life he'd always wanted.

A few days after they decided to ignore their no-sex agreement Soli moved into his bedroom – which he'd suggested, saying it was ridiculous for her to return to her own room every night.

He loved waking up with her beside him. It had been a long time since he'd shared his bed like this, and he was surprised to find how much he'd missed it.

Setting off for the office bright and early one morning, he turned back from opening his car door to see Soli standing on the doorstep, still wearing the short silky pyjamas she looked so damned alluring in, blinking in the sunshine.

'Where are you off to so early?' she asked, carefully picking her way over the gravel towards him in her bare feet.

He met her halfway and lifted her into his arms so she could wrap her legs around his middle and save the soles of her feet from the sharp stones.

Walking back to the car, he put her down gently onto the bonnet and leant in to kiss her, breathing in the enticing, sleep-warmed scent of her.

'I'm off to the office. I want to get everything that needs doing today finished in good time so I can come home early and take you out for dinner. I've booked that new place on Hampstead High Street that you mentioned the other day.'

'Really?' she said, beaming at him. 'That's so thoughtful of you.'

He smiled back. 'It's mostly a selfish move on my part. I really fancied checking it out too.'

Leaning back in, she kissed him hard, and he felt her smile against his lips.

'What are you going to do today?' he asked when they broke apart.

'I'm going to check in on Mum, then go to the cafe. The marketing I've been doing seems to be paying off and we've seen a real increase in business recently.' She took a breath and he felt her fingers dig into his back as she tightened her grip on him. 'And I've decided it's time to give the place a new fit-out.' Her brow pinched in a frown as if she found this idea troubling. 'I can't keep clinging on to my father's vision for the place. It's looking so shabby now and needs modernising.' Her eyes welled with tears. 'Time to let go of the past and look to the future.'

'I think that's a good decision,' he said, running a finger gently under her eye to brush away a tear. His heart gave an extra-hard beat in his chest as it suddenly occurred to him that she was talking about a future he'd have no part in. His time with her would quickly slip away and at some point soon, so would she.

'You know, I think my time with you has really made me grow up and look at life from a new perspective. So thank you for that,' she added with a sad sort of smile.

'I'm glad to have helped,' he said roughly, leaning in again and kissing her hard to try and disguise the troubling emotions that were now raging through him. Emotions he didn't know what to do with.

She let out a small sigh of contentment and pressed herself harder against him.

His mind went mercifully blank. All he wanted to think about right now was the feel of her soft, supple body against his and the luscious, honeyed taste of her in his mouth.

So it was a few seconds before he realised there was someone standing on the driveway with them, clearing his throat to politely get their attention.

Pulling away from Soli, he turned his head to see Samuel Pinker, his great-aunt's spy, looking back at him with a slightly sheepish look on his face.

'Sorry to interrupt you. The front gate was open, so I thought it'd be okay to come right in. I have some documents from your great-aunt's solicitor to drop off and as I was in the area...'

They nodded politely, all of them patently aware that it had actually been another ruse to check up on the two of them, as per Aunt Faith's decree.

'That's quite all right, Mr Pinker,' Soli said with a grin in her voice. 'I was just sending my husband off to work in the best possible way I know.'

Mr Pinker cleared his throat again as a red flush appeared to creep up his neck and brighten his cheeks. 'Your husband's a very lucky man, Mrs McQueen,' he replied. 'And could I just say, I think the two of you make a lovely couple?' He turned to look at Xavier. 'Your great-aunt would be very pleased to see you so happy, Mr McQueen.'

And with those incisive words hanging in the air, he handed the envelope he was carrying to Xavier, gave them both a friendly nod of goodbye and strolled away back towards the open gates.

Soli couldn't help giggling. 'I don't think we need to worry about him thinking we're not behaving like a real married couple any more,' she said with a grin.

Something about the way she said this, on top of Pinker's parting shot, made a shiver of discomfort rush across his skin. Were they acting like a married couple? He wouldn't have said so. They were just enjoying each other's company whilst they were forced to live together. In order to be convincingly married there would have to be a palpable emotional connection between them as well as a physical one. Which he didn't think they had.

Did they?

He mentally shook himself. It wasn't important. They both knew the score. At least, he was pretty sure Soli did. Though from what she'd just said, he was a little worried now that she was allowing herself to become more emotionally attached to him than was wise.

That wasn't what he wanted at all.

Was it?

No. That wasn't what he'd signed up for.

His chest suddenly felt tight.

He needed to get out of there and off to work before his concern became apparent to Soli and potentially started a conflict he really didn't want to deal with right then.

'Anyway, I'll see you later,' he said, forcing himself to give her an unconcerned smile.

'Looking forward to it,' she replied, not seeming to notice the sudden tension in the air. 'Have a good day, darling!'

* * *

Soli strolled back into the house, closed the front door and stopped abruptly in the hallway as a sudden horrifying knowledge that she was going to be sick assaulted her.

Her stomach lurched and churned as she dashed to the nearest bathroom, only just making it there in time.

The bug she'd had in Corsica couldn't have got her again, surely. She'd only had it a few weeks ago.

Was that right?

No. Hang on, it couldn't have been that short a time ago.

Life had been such a whirl; she'd barely had time to notice how the weeks had flown by. It seemed like only yesterday that they'd been in Corsica.

But it wasn't. It was at least six weeks ago.

A cold sensation trickled down her spine as something alarming occurred to her.

She should have had her period by now. She remembered spotting a bit a couple of weeks ago, which wasn't unusual because of the pill she was on, but she'd forgotten to write down when her last proper period was.

Her heart gave a painful thump in her chest and she dragged in a breath as she felt suddenly dizzy.

She couldn't be pregnant though. Could she? They'd used double protection, apart from that time in Corsica when they'd just relied on her pill.

Which she'd not taken for the following two days after they'd had sex because she'd been so ill.

But there was no point panicking. She needed to be sensible and keep a cool head about this.

Pulling herself together, she got dressed then went straight out to the nearest chemist for a pregnancy test, using it as soon as she got home. Just because some things pointed towards her being pregnant, it didn't mean she actually was, she reminded herself as she waited for the results to show. It could be another bug, or stress, or – something else that her whirling brain couldn't think of right now.

The lines appeared in the little window.

It wasn't anything else.

She was pregnant.

Sitting slumped on the bathroom floor, staring at the little white stick in her hand, she felt hot tears press at the backs of her eyes as her stomach dropped to the floor.

This wasn't supposed to happen. This wasn't the plan.

What was Xavier going to say? He'd been so definite about this thing between them being a sex-only arrangement.

But perhaps he'd actually be happy about it, a determined little voice in her head whispered. He'd told her that he'd wanted to have kids before Harriet had left him, after all.

She took some deep breaths and forced herself to calm down.

It could be a wonderful thing for both of them. They were good together. They worked, both in and out of the bedroom. He made her laugh and feel good about herself. She seemed to bring out the best in him. He'd even told her that a couple of times in the last few weeks – perhaps not in those words, but he'd certainly alluded to it. He enjoyed her company, and she his.

But could she really have a child with someone who didn't love her?

Someone who didn't love her as much as she loved him?

Because she knew, in that moment, without a doubt in her mind that there was no point denying it to herself any more.

She was in love with him.

Completely and utterly.

She let out a cynical, broken laugh. So much for being mature enough to deal with a sex-only arrangement. She'd been kidding herself this whole time.

She'd not wanted to admit it to herself before now because she'd been terrified that he didn't feel the same – he was so guarded with his emotions it was difficult to know how he really felt sometimes.

But she knew what she really wanted.

She loved him and wanted them to raise this baby together. For them to stay married after the year was up.

But would he feel the same way?

Could he?

She got up from the floor and brushed herself down with trembling hands.

There was only one way to find out.

* * *

Soli was in the sitting room, anxiously biting her thumbnail, when she finally heard Xavier's car pull into the driveway that evening.

Getting up from the sofa, she went to meet him in the hall on trembling legs. Her heart was racing so hard she felt light-headed.

The door opened and, almost in a dream, she watched Xavier stride inside.

Her stomach flipped right over when he flashed her the smile she loved so much.

'Hi,' he said, dumping his laptop case by the hall table. When he straightened up to look at her the smile fell from his face and was replaced with a concerned frown.

'Are you okay? You look a bit pale. You're not ill again, are you?' He walked towards her and put his hand on her forehead. 'You don't feel hot.'

The compassion of this gesture gave her the confidence to blurt out what she needed to tell him.

'I'm not ill, I'm pregnant.'

It seemed to take him a couple of seconds to process what she'd said, then, shockingly, he took a swift step away from her.

'What?' he said, his voice as hard as stone. 'How? We've been using condoms.' The expression in his eyes was wild as he stared at her in angry denial.

Her heart plummeted, provoking a fresh wave of nausea.

That was not the joyful reaction she'd been hoping for.

She swallowed hard, telling herself he was just in shock and to give him a minute to process it. 'I did a test. It came out positive.' She took it out of her back pocket to show him. 'I think it might have been that night in Corsica.' She dragged in a shaky breath. 'Or maybe one of the condoms failed and my pill wasn't working properly again after I'd been ill.'

He shoved his hand roughly through his hair. 'This wasn't part of the deal, Soli,' he bit out, his voice icy cold and the expression in his eyes so hard it made her shiver.

A feeling of pure dread flooded through her body.

'I take it you want to keep the baby?' he asked.

'Of course I do,' she gasped, horrified that he'd even think for one second that she'd consider not doing so. 'But if you don't want to be involved, I'll find a way to look after it on my own,' she shot back angrily, wounded by his harsh reaction.

'The hell you will,' he snapped.

'What's that supposed to mean?'

'It means there's no way I'm going to abandon my child. Or its mother.'

'But you've been so sure about not wanting to stay married after the year's up,' she pointed out, unable to keep the hurt out of her voice.

He just shrugged. 'We'll work something out. I can speak to Russell and get him to make some amendments to the contract,' he said, his stiff practicality sending little shocks of dismay through her.

'You want us to continue having a contract?' she said, appalled by the thought of it. Had it really come to this? Was he going to keep treating her – and now their child – like a commodity? Just as his parents had done to him?

'Isn't that what every mother wants?' he said coolly. 'To know that she and her child will never have money troubles again?'

His dispassion shocked her. She'd seen him flip into business mode before, but this was a step way beyond that.

'No! That's not what I want! I want a partner who loves me. Who wants to be with me for me. Not because he feels he has to because we have a child together.' She wrapped her arms around her body, aware that she was shaking now. 'We'll only end up resenting each other. It'll be hell living in the same house and I can't let my child grow up in that sort of toxic environment. I can't spend the rest of my life with you if you don't love me back, Xavier. Because I love you!'

He wasn't looking at her now, but down at the floor instead, with a muscle flicking in his jaw.

'Do you love me?' she whispered brokenly, her heart thumping painfully in her throat.

He didn't answer her right away, but even before he opened his mouth to speak, she could tell what he was going to say from the tension in his body language.

'I'm not sure I'm capable of loving anyone any more.'

The expression in his eyes was as hard as marble when he finally looked at her.

Grief squeezed her chest, stealing her breath away.

'If you can't love me, I can't stay here with you any longer,' she said, her voice barely making it past her lips. 'I'll make sure this child has all the love it needs and a happy life, but I'll do it without you and your money.'

She went to sweep past him, but he put out a hand to stop her. 'Soli, don't be ridiculous—'

Her whole body was suddenly hot now. Burning with anger. 'Don't call me ridiculous! I'm sick of hearing that from you. I know you think I'm just some naïve idiot with money problems, but know this: I'm capable of being happier than you'll ever be, because I let people into my heart and treat them with genuine respect – like an equal. If you can't get past that block you have, if you're not willing to, then there's no hope for you, Xavier McQueen. No matter how many houses you own or how much money you have, you'll never be happy if you can't learn to let go and fall in love again, to trust and share your life with someone else. With me!' Her voice broke on the last word, but she fought back the tears, determined not to cry.

Letting out a loud, painful-sounding sigh, he sat down on the edge of the hall table and looked up at her with such cold resentment she felt a shiver run down her spine.

'Where do we go from here?' she whispered, panic rising in her chest.

He frowned and shook his head. 'I don't know, Soli. I just don't know. I don't think I can give you what you want.'

She saw his throat move as he swallowed but his gaze remained implacable.

After what felt like a lifetime of silence, where it became plain he wasn't going to tell her what she needed to hear, she realised the only thing she could do now was get out of there, just so she could calm down and think straight again. She needed to figure out what the hell she was going to do without him.

'Okay. Well, it's clear how you really feel about me.' She coughed to ease the painful tension in her throat. 'So I'm going to go home,' she said shakily, willing herself to hold it together, just for a few more minutes.

He didn't say anything as she turned and walked away. He didn't follow her up to the room they'd shared so happily for the last few weeks, and he wasn't at the front door when she let herself out with a small bag she'd packed.

In short, he made it crystal-clear that he wasn't going to stop her from leaving.

12

GAME OF LIFE – SPIN THE WHEEL OF FATE FOR A CHANCE AT THE LIFE YOU WANT.

It was very quiet in the house once she'd gone.

Xavier paced the floor for what felt like hours, trying to reconcile his thoughts about what Soli had said to him. And what he'd said to her.

Her out-of-the-blue revelation had blindsided him – his harsh words a reaction to the crushing fear that he'd been wrong to relax around her. He'd been totally unprepared for how to handle her unexpected and shocking news, and something dark and instinctive had reared up from deep inside him, making him lash out at her. To protect himself.

The whole time they'd been sleeping together he'd been afraid of this happening, but he'd pushed it away, not wanting to dwell on it, telling himself he was worrying for no reason. He thought he'd been so careful, so clever, using extra protection and making sure they were both on the same page. But he'd forgotten about Corsica. The one weak spot in the whole game.

A restless sort of dread lay heavily in his stomach as he paced around, his veins on fire with adrenaline and terror.

He couldn't give himself fully to her, not in the way she wanted. He'd protected himself from loving anyone else ever since Harriet had torn his heart to shreds and he'd seriously believed he wasn't cut out for that sort of relationship with anyone ever again. He was his parents' son, after all.

And he'd managed to keep his feelings under control and his heart protected, until Soli had come along and turned his world upside down.

Letting her in had been such a gradual process, he'd barely noticed it. He thought they were just having fun, but from the way he was feeling now that she'd walked out on him, it was clear she'd worked her way firmly into his affections.

He spent a rough night, barely sleeping a wink, Soli's sweet scent on his sheets haunting his dreams when he did sleep.

Getting up groggy and tired the next day, with his head heavy and tight with stress, he made his way down to the kitchen in the hope that a strong cup of coffee would help him think straight.

Just the sight of the empty room where he and Soli had spent so much time enjoying each other's company made him want to punch a wall in frustrated regret.

What was he going to do? How would he handle this? He suddenly desperately wanted her to be there to talk to – to see her kind, reassuring smile again. Supporting him. Caring for him.

Not that she was ever likely to be doing that again after the way he'd treated her.

Did he really believe he couldn't love her?

He didn't know any more – his head felt as if it was stuffed with cotton wool, and his blood was like sludge in his veins.

Dropping his head into his hands, he let out a loud, frustrated sigh and sank back against the work surface, feeling the hard ridge of it digging in to his spine, but he didn't move; instead, he revelled in the pain it caused him, glad of the distraction from the more problematic pain in his heart.

* * *

The next few days were hell.

Soli kept her word, staying away from the house, and from him.

He'd thought it would be okay, that it would be hard but he'd be able to cope without her there – but he felt sick every time he came downstairs and found she still hadn't returned. The house was so silent and dark without her, as if she'd taken all the life and colour of the place with her when she left.

Most distressingly, the house no longer felt like his home.

There was a constant, tight ache in his chest – which he accepted, when he finally allowed himself to acknowledge it, was because he missed her.

He missed her like crazy.

The following Saturday he woke up early, the sense of doom he'd been carrying around with him since she'd gone weighing on him more heavily than ever.

Once downstairs he found he couldn't settle to anything. It was too quiet, too still in the house, so he grabbed his jacket and walked to Hampstead Village in search of something to distract him.

He was just passing some seating outside a coffee house when he heard someone calling his name. Turning to see who it was, he felt his pulse leap as he saw Harriet sitting in one of the chairs, cradling a tightly swaddled baby.

'Harriet. How are you?' he asked, his voice a little unsteady with a strange kind of yearning that had swelled in him at the sight of the child in her arms.

'I'm really well, thanks. Meet Harry, my son,' she said, beaming down towards the baby.

'Hello, Harry,' Xavier said, bending down to look more closely at the tiny human in her arms, fighting back an intense surge of emotion that was threatening to engulf him.

Would his and Soli's child be a boy? he wondered wildly, his heart thumping hard at the thought.

'Where's Soli?' Harriet asked, as if sensing his turmoil.

'She's at home,' he lied, standing up straight again, pain throbbing hard through his chest at the sound of her name.

'I guess the two of you might be having your own little bundle of joy soon,' Harriet said with a twinkle in her eye. 'I always thought you'd make a fabulous father, despite what I said all those years ago.' She appeared to swallow and blink, as if suddenly uncomfortable. 'Listen, I just wanted to say sorry for the way I treated you back then,' she went on before he could respond. 'It was an incredibly selfish way to behave.' Her smile was full of what looked like genuine regret now. 'I was afraid you didn't really love me for me, you just thought I ticked all the boxes for the sort of woman you thought you should be marrying.' She hugged her son a little tighter to her. 'But I guess it all worked out for the best. You and Soli looked so happy together when I saw you at the party.'

'We were,' he said, realising with a shock that he was actually speaking the truth now. He had been happy then. 'And I forgive you for what happened with us. You were right; we wouldn't have been good for each other. We probably would have made each other miserable.'

And he really meant that too.

Because he recognised now that Soli was right for him. She'd brought him back from the brink of despair and helped him realise that he wasn't like his parents at all; that he was capable of loving someone other than himself. Soli made him happy because she truly cared about him, for him, just as Great-Aunt Faith had. The warmth that the two most important women in his life had bestowed on him had instinctively made him feel secure. Wanted.

Loved.

Which was what he'd really been trying to hang on to all along. Not the house, but the security he'd thought it had represented.

He turned away from Harriet to stare at the empty space beside him, remembering how he'd grown used to turning to find Soli smiling at him – and how it had felt like being given a shot of adrenaline straight to his heart.

His life was empty without her.

Dragging in a deep, fortifying breath, he turned to glance in the opposite direction, towards the rental units he owned on the High Street, suddenly so clearly knowing exactly what he wanted.

He wanted Soli back. And he wanted their child too. He wanted them to be a family – something he'd always longed for but had previously accepted he'd never have. Until now. Until her.

So what the hell was he doing still standing there?

Blood pulsing hard through his body, he said goodbye to Harriet and started off in the direction of the board game cafe. He was going to talk this thing out with Soli once and for all. Exactly what he was going to say, he wasn't sure, but he felt confident it would come to him as soon as he set eyes on her.

He knew some sort of grand gesture was in order if he had any chance of winning her back though. He'd done too much damage with his selfish silence to just expect her to listen to his demands.

She was too self-possessed for that.

He needed to find a way to prove to her that he was genuinely sorry and that he meant it when he told her he couldn't live without her. That he wanted them to be a real family, something he'd never had before – had never felt worthy of – but had ached for his whole life.

But what if she turned him down? What if she just laughed in his face?

His pace slowed as the idea rattled through him, and he stopped and leant a hand against the window of the nearest shop as a dark kind of fear seized him.

That was probably what he deserved after the way he'd treated her, but could he really put himself through that sort of humiliation again? It had nearly killed him the last time it had happened to him.

On the other hand, was he really prepared to lose everything he'd ever wanted because he was too afraid he might lose it later? That made no sense at all. His damn stupid pride was getting in the way of his happiness, and Soli's too, and he couldn't allow that to happen. She was the only person that had never let him down.

She loved him. That was abundantly clear.

And he knew without a doubt that she'd make an incredible mother to his child and the most loving, caring partner he could ever hope for.

Even if he struggled to get the loving thing right, he knew that Soli would be there the whole way, backing him up and evening him out. They would make a brilliant team.

He wanted her back. The woman who had helped him live again and appreciate everything he had for more than just its monetary worth.

The woman who made him happy.

The woman he loved.

He knew for absolute certain now that the house meant nothing to him if she wasn't in it. It was just bricks and mortar, full of ghosts and regrets – an empty shell without her.

She, and her love and affection, was what he'd really needed all along.

The house was his past, but she was his future. She and their baby.

With unwavering resolve making his heart thump hard in his chest, he started walking swiftly towards the cafe again, prepared to do everything in his power to save their marriage.

He was in love with Soli and he was going to do whatever it took to prove it to her.

* * *

Soli was practically dead on her feet.

She'd not slept properly since leaving Xavier's house – the place she'd previously begun to consider her home too until she'd been made to feel supremely unwelcome there – and it was really beginning to show.

Even her mother had noticed her lack of energy and positivity in the last few days.

Xavier's initial, shocked reaction to the pregnancy had been understandable – she recognised that – but to reject her love, then let her leave and not contact her again, was just plain heartless.

To be perfectly honest, it had broken her heart.

But then, she'd not contacted him either, she accepted with a thud of despair. She'd been too afraid to, in case she saw that look of cool reproach on his face again.

Sighing loudly, she picked up a mug from a tray of newly washed crockery and rubbed the tea towel over it. It was all very well holing herself up here, but she was going to have to face him again eventually so they could work this thing out between them. She'd signed a contract to stay married to him for the next few months after all and there was no way she was going to welch on their deal. She wasn't a quitter.

She was just finishing this thought when a familiar and stomach-twisting scent hit her senses.

Looking up, she found herself staring into the dark intensity of Xavier's gaze.

'Hi, Soli,' he said quietly.

'What are you doing here?' she blurted, completely losing any poise she'd coached herself to exude when next confronted with him.

'I came to talk to you.'

'Here?' she said, glancing around her, unable to keep the incredulity out of her voice.

The corner of his mouth twitched up. 'Yes. I figured it's as good a place as any.'

'It's not exactly private,' she said, gesturing round at the tables full of customers and at her sister and mother, who were currently drinking coffee at the other end of the bar, celebrating a successful end to Domino's first term at university. The two women were now watching them, their interest clearly piqued.

'That's my sister and mother over there,' Soli hissed under her breath so they wouldn't hear her.

'Have you told them about us?' he asked.

'No. Not yet.'

He gave a sharp nod, but didn't move away from the counter. 'Well, we could go somewhere a bit quieter if you like.'

Suddenly she didn't want to move away from behind the counter. She wanted to make him pay for his indifference towards her by forcing him to say whatever he had to say in front of all these people. To hell with his manly pride. She didn't need to take his feelings into consideration any more, especially when he obviously had no intention of protecting hers.

'No. Whatever you have to say to me you can do right here. I'm busy doing my job – I don't have time to leave just so you can reject me again.' She folded her arms and stared him down, determined not to let him win this time.

She might love him, much more than she was willing to admit right now, but she was damned if she was going to let him hurt her any more than he already had.

She and the baby would be fine without him and his money. She had enough love in her to count for two parents.

Out of the corner of her eye she noticed her sister was still staring at them both.

'Soli, did this guy break your heart or something? Is that why you've been moping around looking so broken since I got back?' Domino called out.

Obviously, they weren't being as discreet as she'd hoped.

She swallowed and was about to answer when Xavier spoke over her.

'Yes, I'm afraid I did. And I came here to apologise and tell your sister how much I love and miss her.'

He turned back to face her and looked directly into her eyes.

She just stood there, dumbstruck, with blood rushing in her ears, wondering if she'd misheard him.

'I'm sorry,' he said, with such emotion in his voice she knew immediately that he genuinely meant it. 'I'm so sorry for hurting you.' He put his hands on the counter and leant in closer to her. 'I don't work properly without you. You've changed me, changed the way I think about life and what love really is. I don't deserve you, Soli, I know that, but I want you back. I want us all to be a family.'

'Really?' was all she could think to reply to that, her scrambled brain slow to catch up with everything he was saying.

'Yes. Really. I got spooked when you told me about the baby because I'd promised myself I wouldn't fall for you, and it made me realise that I had. That I wanted you more than I should. I've been a complete idiot. You're the best thing that's ever happened to me – you and the baby.'

There was a loud gasp and a squeal from the direction of her mother and sister, but Soli ignored it, her attention focused solely on Xavier now.

'You really want me back?' she asked shakily.

'Yes,' he said with more determination in his voice than she'd ever heard before. He moved round to the opening in the counter and took her hand in his, gently tugging on it to ask her to follow him out to the floor of the cafe.

When they were both standing in front of the now mostly silent room – since the whole of the clientele appeared to have stopped playing their games to stare at them instead – Xavier dropped to one knee and looked up at her with such intensity in his eyes her heart nearly flew out of her body with excitement. His hand was shaking as he held onto hers tightly, their palms pressed hard together, and she realised with a shock that he was scared. He was afraid she would reject him, but he was still going through with this, in front of all these people.

He wasn't hiding any more.

He swallowed, looking as though he was having trouble starting his sentence, but his voice was loud and clear when he spoke. 'As you're aware, I find it really hard to trust people, but I know – I guess I've always known, deep down – that I can trust you, Soli. I love the idea of you being the mother of my child. You're the most wonderful, caring, compassionate person I've ever met, and it would be a huge privilege to spend the rest of my life with you.'

There was a low murmur from the crowd, but he didn't let it distract him.

'I promise you, I will do everything in my power to make you happy. I'll give you everything I have, everything, if you'll come back home with me.'

She could barely breathe as the reality of his words began to sink in.

'I love you, Solitaire McQueen. Will you marry me,' he paused and smiled before adding, 'for real this time?'

Soli thought her heart might explode with happiness.

Xavier loved her and he wanted them all to be a family. A real family.

'I love you too,' she sobbed, unable to control her emotions any longer. 'And yes,' she took a steadying breath, 'I'll marry you.' She grinned through her tears. 'Again.'

He kissed her hand before standing up and pulling her into his arms, where he held her to him so tightly she could barely breathe, before finally drawing away just far enough to kiss her deeply, with the love and emotion she'd always known he had in him.

'We'll make one hell of a team, Mrs McQueen,' he murmured against her lips, and she knew, right then, that there would be no more games.

She'd won the ultimate prize.

EPILOGUE
BINGO – HOLD YOUR NERVE FOR THE ULTIMATE PRIZE.

Five years later

'Found you!' came the excited voice of four-year-old Faith McQueen as she pulled back the curtain to reveal her mother crouched on the window seat behind it.

'Darn! And I thought I had the perfect hiding place,' Soli said with a grin, ruffling the hair of her eldest daughter and pulling her in for a kiss.

'Mum, let go – I still need to find Dad and Joy,' Faith said, struggling out of her arms, but not before dabbing one last wet kiss on Soli's cheek.

'Okay, go ahead,' Soli said, unfolding herself from her cramped position with a sigh of relief and heading back to the kitchen, where she still had some last-minute preparations to do for Xavier's birthday meal.

She'd made one of her famous chocolate fudge cakes for dessert and she needed to get it out of the oven now so it'd be absolutely perfect.

It wasn't long before Xavier came striding in through the door with two-year-old Joy on his shoulders and Faith clinging around his waist with her feet on top of his, doing the penguin walk.

'You seem to have a new hat and pair of trousers,' she joked. 'Did you get them for your birthday?'

She laughed as Xavier shot her a rueful look while he tried, and failed, to prise his children off him.

He was amazing with them, as Soli had always suspected he would be, and they'd both become real Daddy's girls to prove her right. He clearly adored them and had even hinted he'd be very happy to have more kids if she thought she might too.

'Where's everyone else?' Faith asked, her eyes round with excitement when she saw the kitchen table laden with the special birthday meal.

She was talking, in part, about Soli's mother, who had moved in with them and taken the downstairs bedroom when her Parkinson's had worsened and it had become impossible for her to manage stairs. It was a great arrangement because it meant the girls could spend lots of time with their grandmother, and she absolutely adored having them around her. She often said to Soli that they kept her young.

After acing her degree at Oxford, Domino had gone on to do a master's in pure maths and was now starting a PhD at King's College London. She'd moved in with them last year – eventually bringing her boyfriend too, another PhD student from her department, who was deeply devoted to Soli's brilliant sister. If the two of them had kids, Soli suspected they'd be so smart they'd go on to solve all six of the remaining mathematical Millennium prize projects or something.

The house was no longer the silent show home it had been when she'd first moved in. It was now always full of life and laughter, which Xavier happily asserted would have delighted his great-aunt Faith, and openly admitted that he loved too.

Soli had sold the business on to another board game enthusiast when she fell pregnant for the second time and had decided she wanted to be able to spend more time at home with both the children and her mother. She didn't regret it for a second. It had always been her father's dream really, and it had been high time she'd chased her own.

To that end, she'd enrolled in college to study fashion design, something she'd really enjoyed at school, and was now in the process of setting up her own clothing line, which she'd decided to call Solitaire.

It was all up for grabs, which was exactly the way she'd come to like it.

'Speaking of birthday presents,' she said to Xavier once he'd finally freed himself from his daughters' vice-like grip.

'You know I didn't want you to get me anything.' He gave her a mock-stern frown, then pulled her hard against his body, wrapping his arms around her. 'Just this,' he said, dropping his mouth to hers for a long, sweet kiss.

'Well, I'm afraid I ignored your instructions,' she teased, when they finally broke apart, flashing him a smile.

He let out a long, fake sigh. 'Why am I not surprised?'

'I thought you might like this though,' she said, pulling out a long, flat package.

He frowned, taking it from her and pulling off the wrapping paper to reveal a pregnancy testing kit.

'You're pregnant again?' he asked, his eyes lighting up with excitement.

'I am,' she said, grinning as he pulled her back against him and planted little kisses all over her face.

'Well, that's the best birthday present I've ever had,' he said gruffly, grinning from ear to ear.

'You realise there are going to be even more years of hide-and-seek to get through now,' she joked, laughing as he began to kiss down her neck.

'That works for me,' he said, his voice muffled against her skin. 'I know all the best hiding places in this house now.'

She smiled, thinking how much he'd changed since she'd first met him. He was so full of love and happiness with his place in the world now, she barely recognised the withdrawn, emotionally scarred man he'd been then.

Contentment swelled in her chest as she looked at her family gathered around her.

Right at that moment she couldn't have been happier. She had everyone she loved right there with her and an exciting future stretching ahead with Xavier by her side.

A future she was no longer afraid to face.

She was proud of the brave, strong and confident person she'd become, thanks to Xavier's belief in her.

In fact, they'd made a pact that there would be no more hiding from life – for either of them – ever again.

He'd been absolutely right: they made the perfect team.

* * *

MORE FROM CHRISTY McKELLEN

You can order the next sparkling, spicy romantic comedy from Christy McKellen here:

https://mybook.to/NewMcKellenBackAd

ABOUT THE AUTHOR

Christy McKellen is the author of provocative and sexy romance novels that have sold over half a million copies worldwide.

Download your exclusive bonus content from Christy McKellen here:

Visit Christy's website: www.christymckellen.com

Follow Christy on social media here:

[f] facebook.com/christymckellenauthor
[X] x.com/ChristyMcKellen
[O] instagram.com/christymckellen
[BB] bookbub.com/authors/christy-mckellen

ALSO BY CHRISTY MCKELLEN

Three's a Crowd

Marry Me...Maybe?

About Last Night

Best Mistake Ever

Here Comes Trouble

So That Happened

The Paradise Hook-Up

Best Laid Plans

I Do, For Now

Boldwood
EVER AFTER
x♡x♡

JOIN BOLDWOOD'S
**ROMANCE
COMMUNITY**
FOR SWEET AND
SPICY BOOK RECS
WITH ALL YOUR
FAVOURITE
TROPES!

SIGN UP TO OUR
NEWSLETTER

HTTPS://BIT.LY/BOLDWOODEVERAFTER

Boldwood

Boldwood Books is an award-winning fiction publishing company seeking out the best stories from around the world.

Find out more at www.boldwoodbooks.com

Join our reader community for brilliant books, competitions and offers!

Follow us
@BoldwoodBooks
@TheBoldBookClub

Sign up to our weekly deals newsletter

https://bit.ly/BoldwoodBNewsletter

www.ingramcontent.com/pod-product-compliance
Lightning Source LLC
Chambersburg PA
CBHW011801010726
47497CB00012B/3228